WALT DISNEY STUDIOS PRESENTS

A STUDIO GHIBLI FILM

My Neighbor TOTORO Picture Book

Original Story and Screenplay Written and Directed by

Hayao Miyazaki

VIZ Media
San Francisco

Meet the characters

Mei Kusakabe
An energetic and adventurous four-year-old girl.

Satsuki Kusakabe
Mei's bright and responsible older sister. A fourth grader.

Dad
Tatsuo Kusakabe
The girls' father is a university professor.

Mom
Yasuko Kusakabe
The girls' mother. She is sick and has been in the hospital for a year.

Kanta Ogaki
Satsuki's classmate.

Granny
Kanta's grandmother.

Totoro and Friends

Totoro

Totoros are creatures that have lived in Japan for longer than humans have. They exist peacefully in the forest, eating acorns and other nuts. Humans usually cannot see them. Totoros sleep during the day and play their ocarinas (round flutes) on moonlit nights. They can even fly. Mei is the one who came up with the name "Totoro."

Big Totoro
About 1300 years old. Almost 7 feet tall!

Medium Totoro
About 600 years old.

Little Totoro
About 100 years old.

Cat Bus
The Cat Bus gives rides to the Totoros. Most humans can't see the Cat Bus, but they do feel a strong gust of wind when it passes by. With its twelve legs, it can even fly in the sky and run on water.

Susuwatari
(Soot Gremlins, Soot Sprites)
Mischievous little balls of dust.

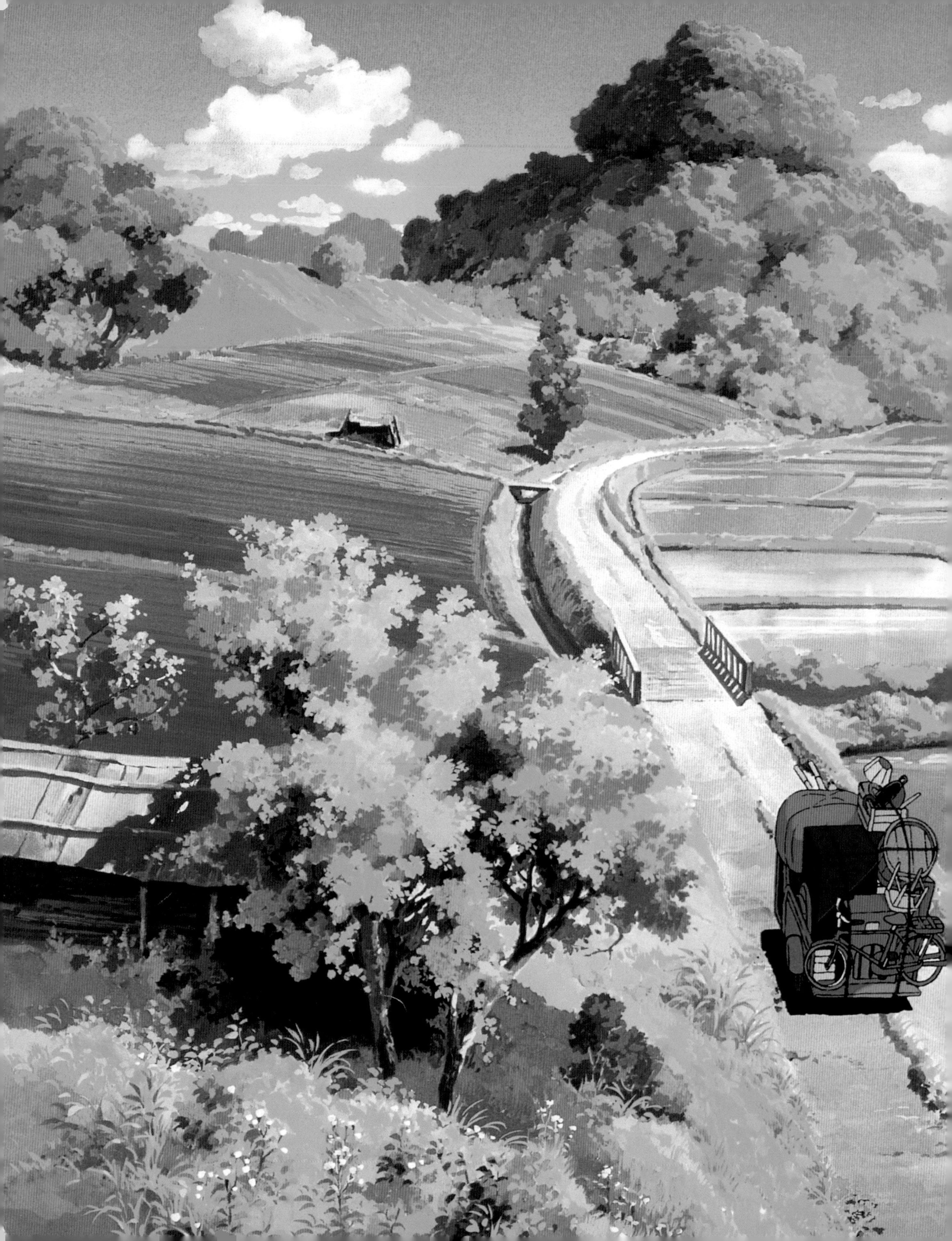

Vroom, vroom, rattle, rattle. A little truck loaded with all kinds of luggage bounced down the bumpy country road.

It was a sunny Sunday in May, and sisters Satsuki and Mei were moving to a new village.

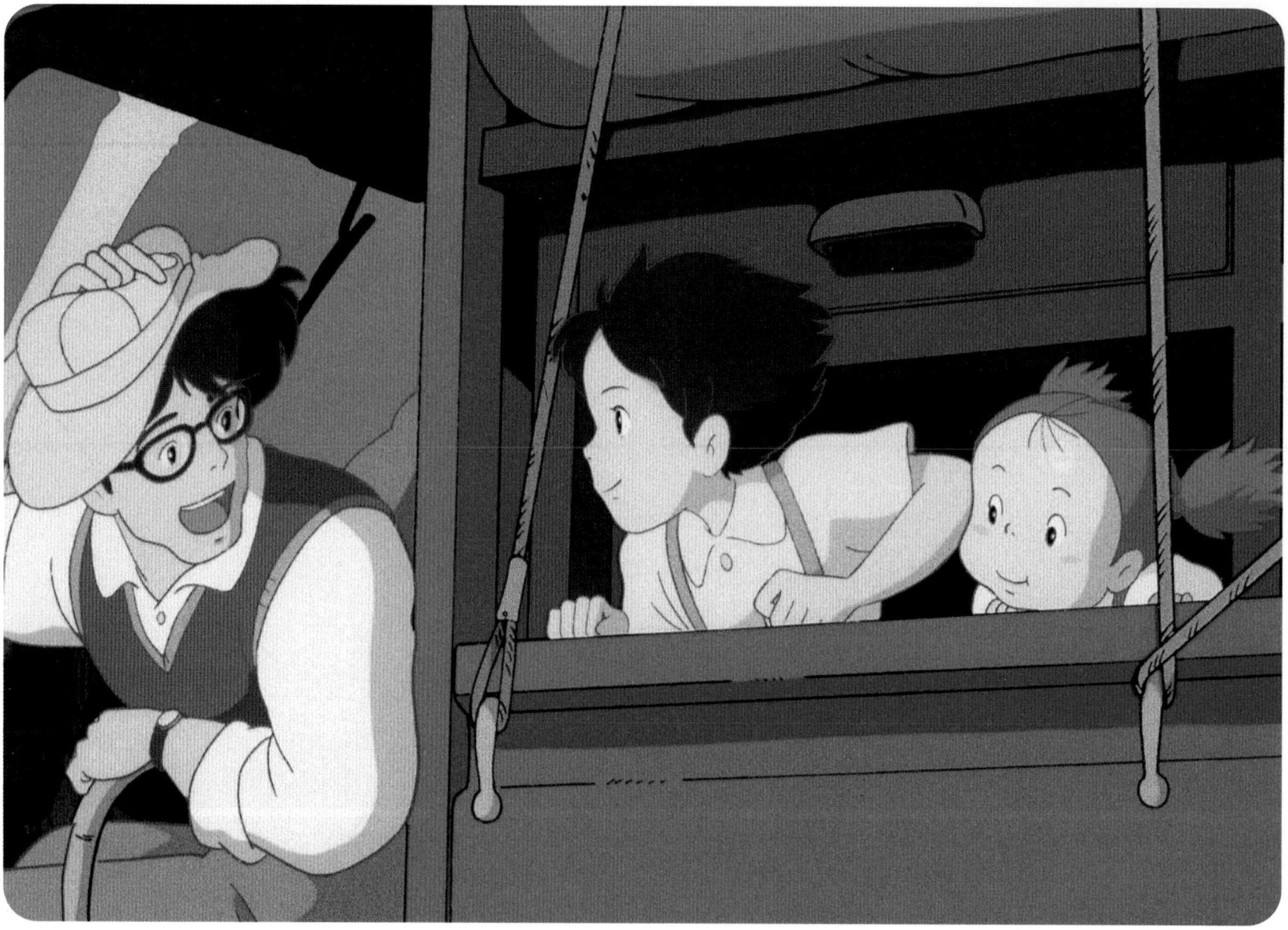

The Haunted House

"It's so pretty here, Dad!" exclaimed Satsuki.

"Yeah, Dad!" Mei chimed in.

The rice paddies, vegetable fields, and the great green forest all seemed to promise the beginning of a wonderful adventure. The girls were very excited.

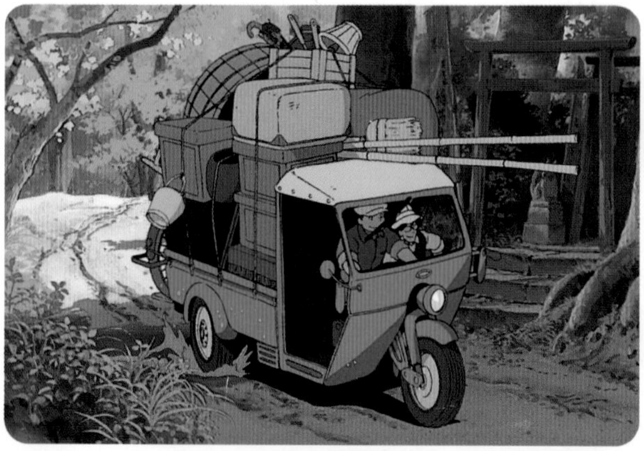

The moment Dad said "This is it, girls," Satsuki and Mei ran off to explore. On the far side of an overgrown garden stood a tattered old house. It looked like nobody had lived there for years.

"Wow. It's creepy!"

"Creepy!" echoed Mei.

"It looks like it could be haunted."

"Haunted?!"

But both girls fell in love with the old country house right away.

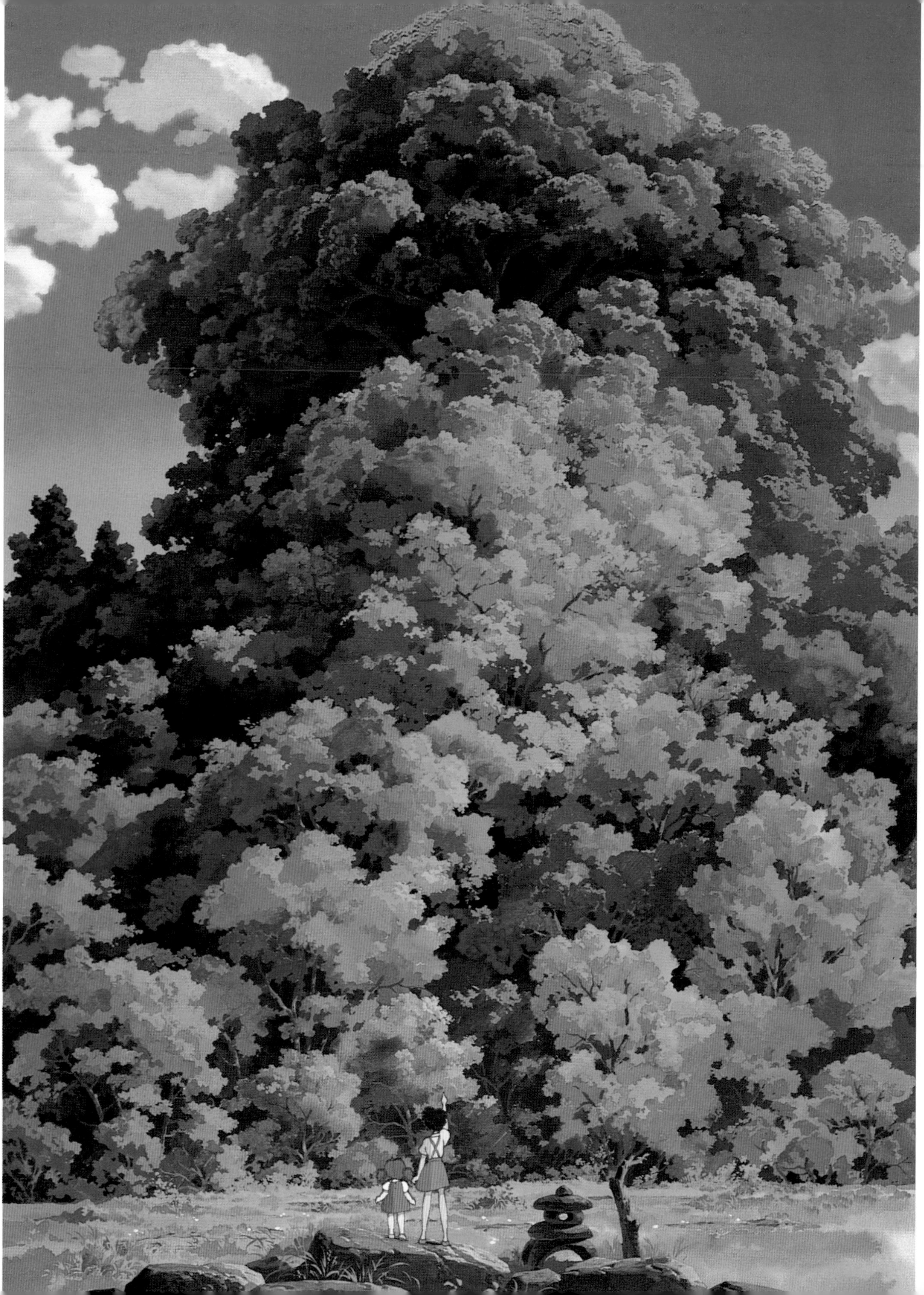

"Mei, look!" Satsuki pointed to the forest next to the house. At the top was a very big tree. "It's huge, isn't it?"

"That's a camphor tree," explained Dad as he opened the shutters to the house.

He handed Satsuki some keys. "Will you open the back of the house?"

Satsuki and Mei ran to the back of the house, ready to work. They opened a rusty old lock.

It's so dark in here, Satsuki thought. Just then, a huge swarm of furry black clumps scurried away towards the far side of the kitchen!

"Did you see that?" Satsuki whispered.

"Yeah. Were they ghosts?" Mei whispered back.

The two looked at each other, then screamed at the top of their lungs.

"Ahhhhhhhh!"
The kitchen now looked quiet. The girls cautiously crept inside, but the room seemed empty.

Dad found them peering around.
"Back to work, now. Let's open the
windows upstairs next. I wonder
where the stairs are?"

"There's an upstairs?" asked Mei.

"We'll find the stairs!" shouted
Satsuki. The girls raced off in
search of the stairs.

"Mei, I found the stairs!"

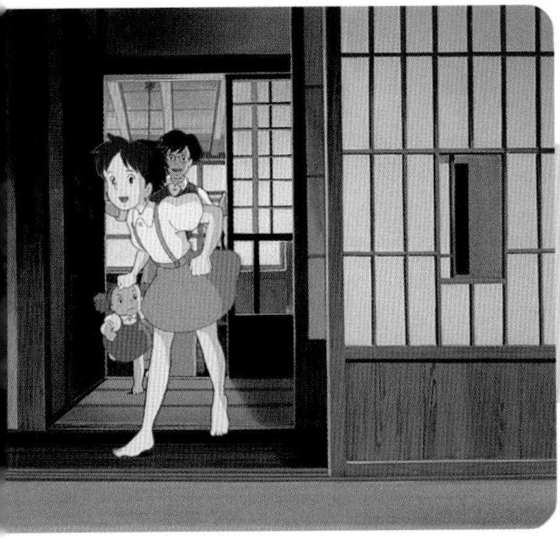

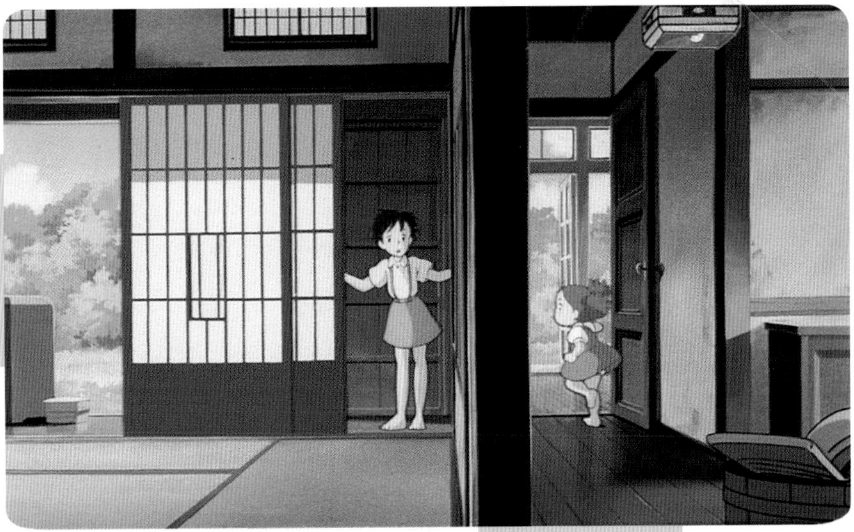

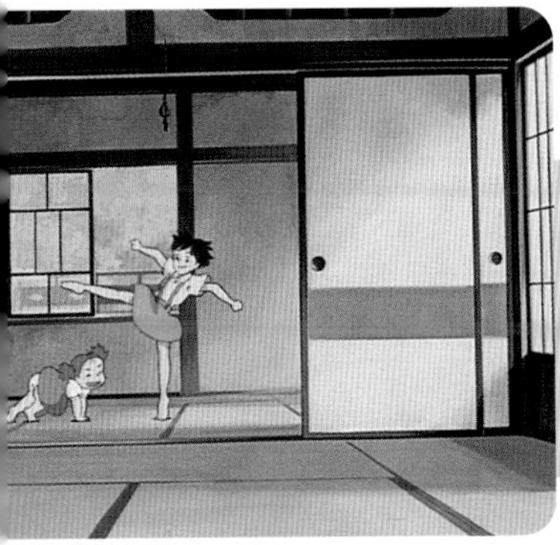

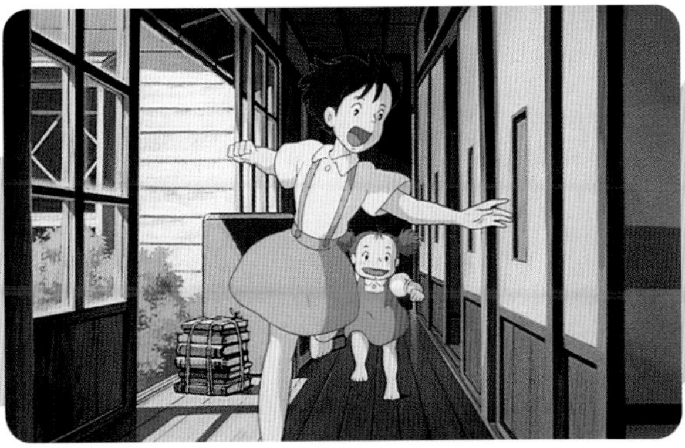

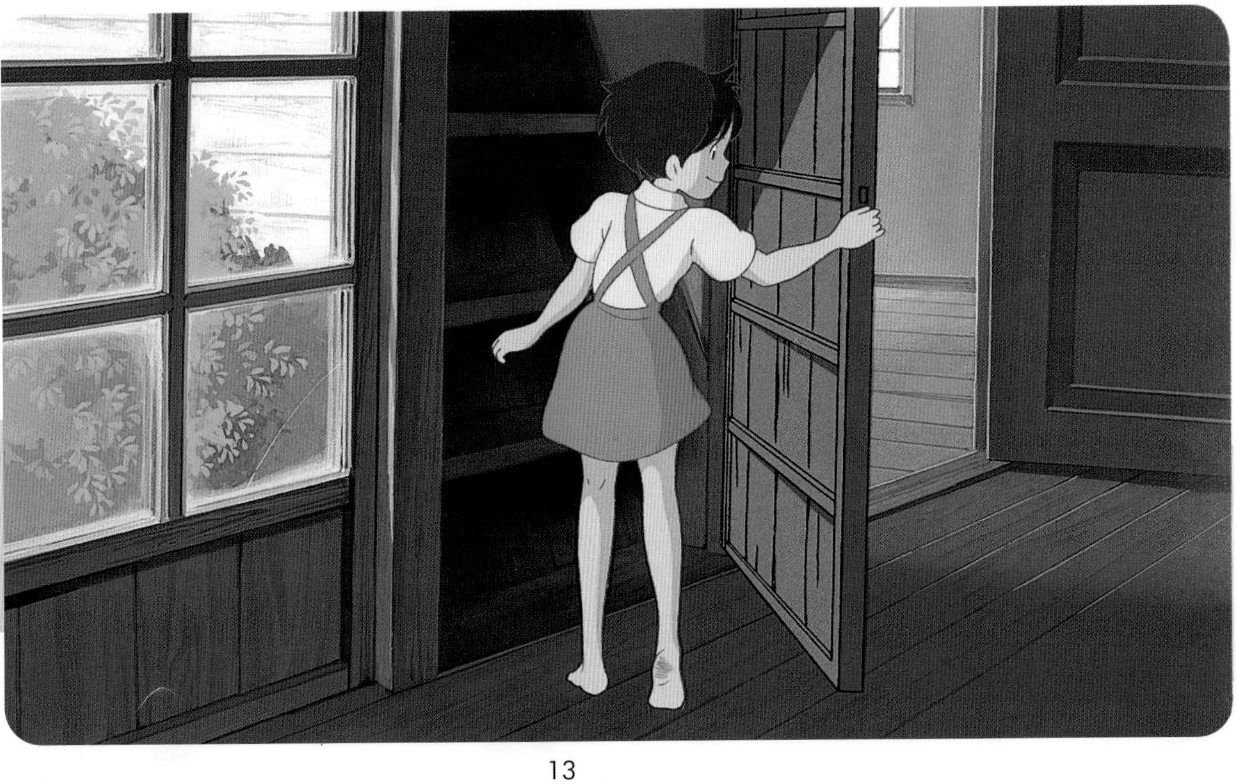

Satsuki and Mei stared up the dark stairway.

Suddenly, something small came falling down the stairs
from above.
Tonk, tonk, tonk.
It was an acorn. Something was up there! The girls
peered into the darkness.

"Mei, let's go see."

"Okay."

Upstairs it was pitch dark. They couldn't see a thing. Satsuki hurried to open a window. The old shutters went *creeeak*.

As soon as the bright sunlight streamed into the room, *fwooosh!* A swarm of little black balls scurried to the back of the room.

"Here they are again!" Mei turned toward the back wall.

Outside, Dad was busy unloading the luggage.

"Dad! There's something weird in this house!"
Dad heard Satsuki and looked up at the window. "That's great. I've wanted to live in a haunted house ever since I was a little boy."

"Aah!" Dad almost tripped carrying a large dresser.

"Oops, I'd better go help," said Satsuki, and she ran downstairs.

Mei stayed behind, her gaze
fixed on the back wall. What
could it be? What could it be?

She walked slowly toward the
wall and poked her finger into a
crack.

Whooosh!

A whole bunch of fuzzy little black balls flew out and escaped into a crack in the ceiling. Mei stood still in surprise. She watched as one fuzzy black ball drifted softly down in front of her.

Somehow that one had not
escaped with the others.

One…two…*clap!* Mei caught it
in her hands.

"Satsuki, look!" She hurried down
the stairs.

Mei ran so fast that she bumped smack into somebody. It was an old woman she'd never seen before.

"Girls, this is Granny from next door. She's come to help."

Mei was too excited to listen to Dad. She opened her hands slowly, but they were empty! Her hands were black with dust. So were the bottoms of her feet.

"Mine are black, too!" Satsuki discovered.

"Oh, my my," warbled Granny. "You've got soot
sprites in your house. They live in old, empty
houses and run all over the place covering
everything with dust and dirt. Don't worry, they're nothing to be
afraid of. After a while they'll just go away."

A boy appeared at the back door. It was Kanta, from next door.

"Ma said to give this to Granny," he said with a scowl.

Kanta handed a wooden basket to Satsuki and ran off.

"Hey, wait," Satsuki called out.

Kanta turned around and shouted back, "Your house is haunted!"

Satsuki stuck her tongue out at him. "Who asked you?!"

But when she looked into the basket Kanta brought, it was full of sweet rice cakes.

23

Satsuki and Mei finally
finished moving in.

Rustle rustle.
That evening the soot sprites
moved, too. They floated
softly up toward the forest on
the night breeze.

Whooo, whooo.

Mysterious hoots could be
heard coming from the forest.
Was it an owl?

The next day Satsuki, Mei and Dad went to visit Mom in the hospital.

Soon Mom would be able to leave the hospital. The family had moved to the countryside because the fresh, clean air would be good for her.

"I'm so happy to see you girls! So how do you like the new house?" asked Mom.

"Pssst, pssst." Satsuki whispered.

Mom smiled brightly. "A haunted house?"

"Mm-hmm. Mommy, do you like haunted houses?" asked Mei worriedly.

"Of course. I'll have to get better soon so I can meet some ghosts," Mom replied as she brushed Satsuki's hair.

The girls loved the house even more after hearing that. They could hardly wait for the day when their mother would come home.

Mei Meets Totoro

One day, Mei was playing by herself. Satsuki was at school and Dad was busy working.

"Huh? An acorn!" Mei found one, then another. They led to a whole trail of acorns.

Mei was excited. She picked up each acorn.

Just then she noticed two small, white, pointy things. They were coming toward her through the grass.

"Hmm?"

It was a strange creature she had never seen before. What could it be?! Mei was curious. She followed it eagerly.

This surprised the white creature, and it scampered away.

"Wait!"

The creature trotted along and then disappeared under the house.

Mei squatted down to stare at it. Behind her, something crept along softly.

"Hey! Now there are two!"
Mei ran after them. The two creatures
quickly fled into the bushes.

There was a tunnel! The tunnel led through
the bushes.

Mei hurried to follow the pointy-eared
creatures. She lost her hat and got her clothes all
dirty, but she didn't even notice.

When they reached the trunk of a big tree, the two
creatures disappeared.

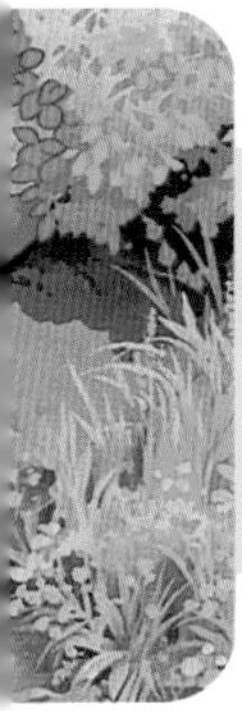
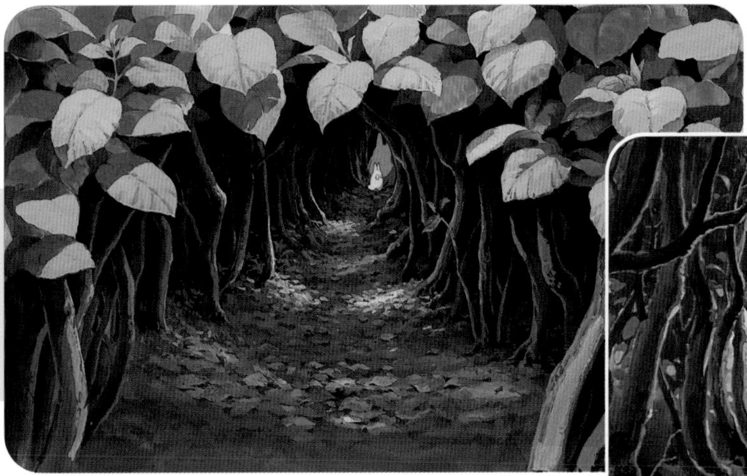
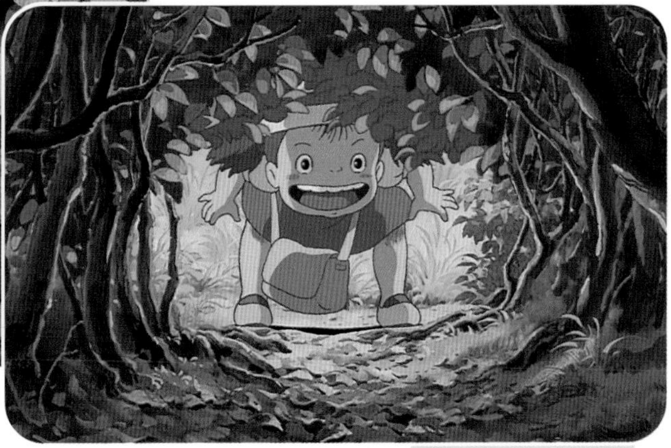
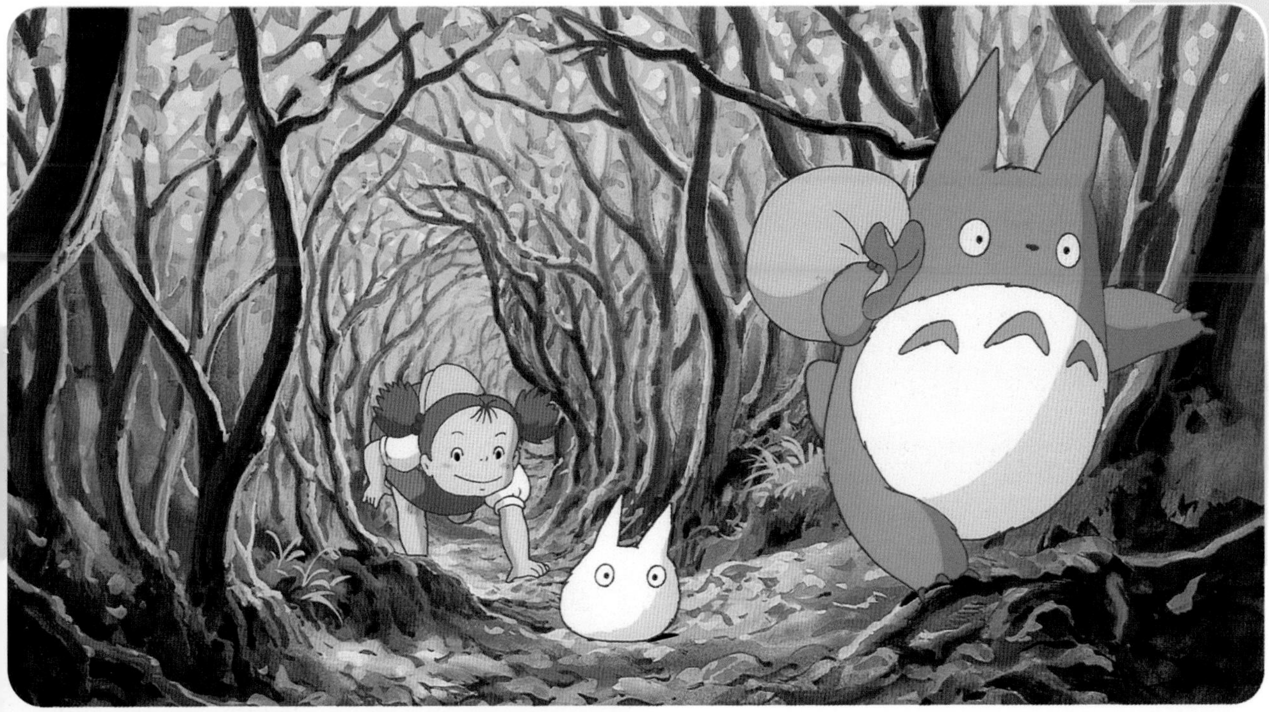
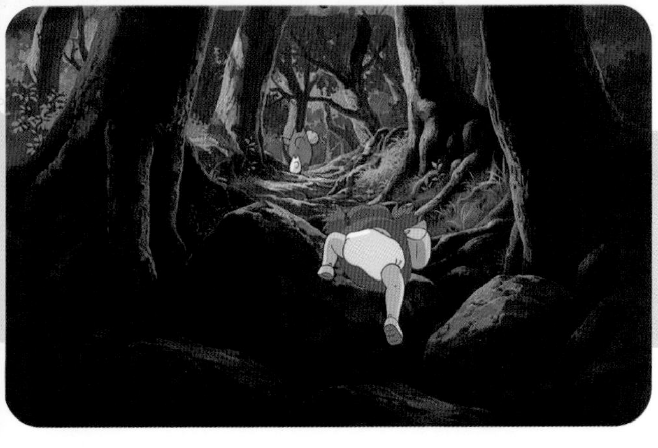
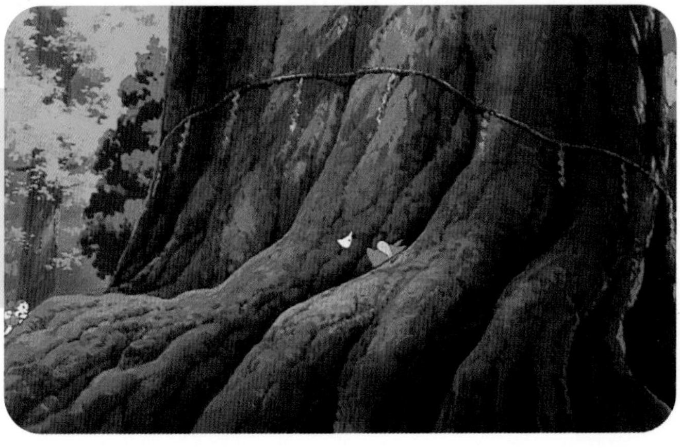

By the roots of the tree there was a dark hole. Next to it lay an acorn.

Mei reached out to get the acorn, but her foot slipped.

"Ahhhhh!"

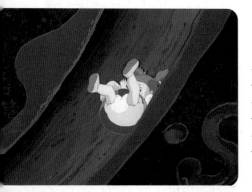

Thud. What a surprise! What a strange place! Even though she was inside a tree, there was light shining in from above. Everything around her glowed green.

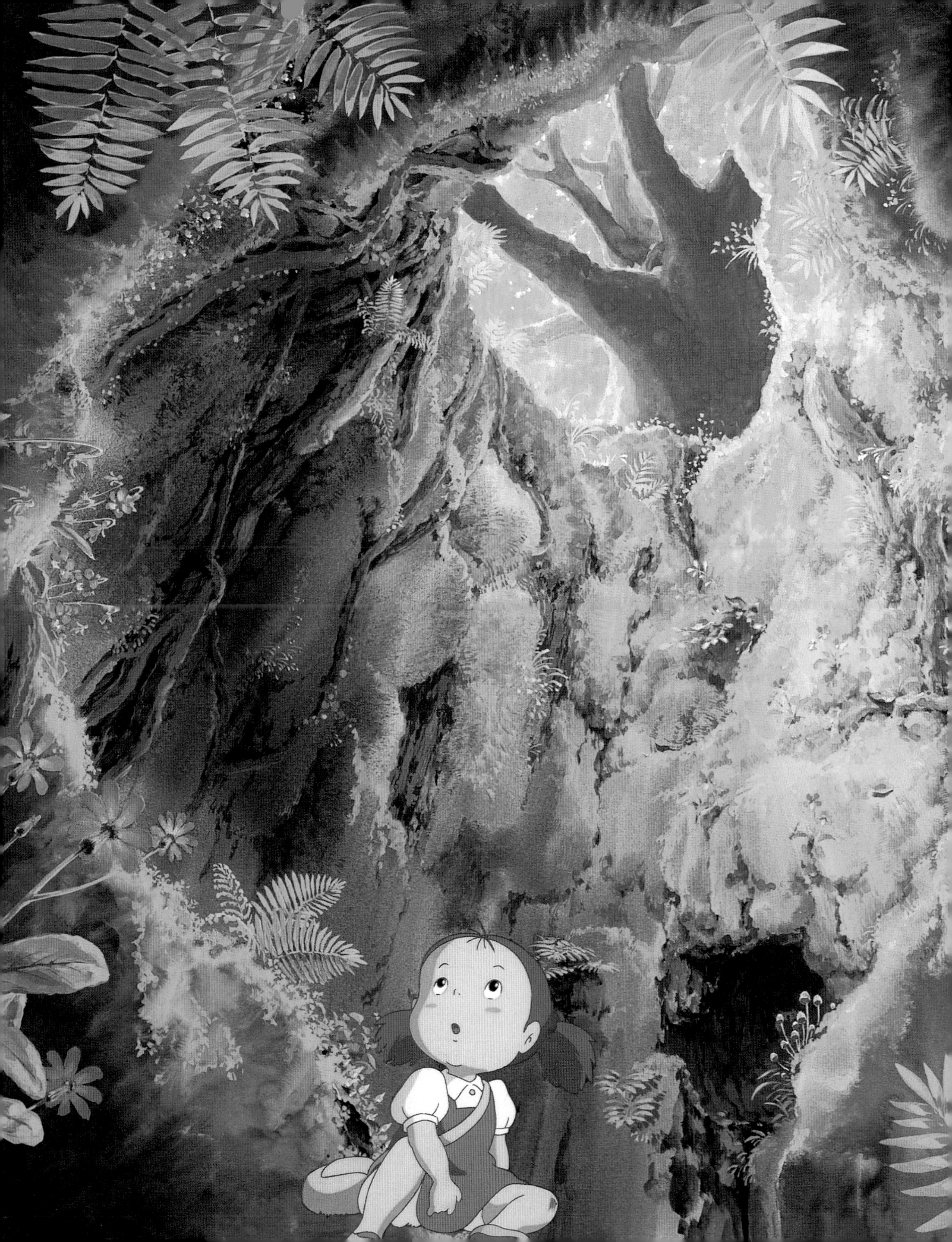

Even more surprising was the enormous creature sleeping there. It was even bigger than the first two she'd seen. The mysterious

creature looked like a cross between a bear and a raccoon and an owl.

Mei opened her eyes wide and approached it slowly.

"Who are you?" she asked.

The mysterious creature slowly opened its eyes.

It seemed very sleepy, indeed.

It twitched its nose, then opened its wide mouth and spoke. "Do-do-rooooooo."

What a wide mouth! A strong gust
of wind came from the mouth.

"Ahh! I'm going to be blown off!"

Mei was so excited. She roared, too.
"Gwaaaaah!"

"Do-Do-roooooo."

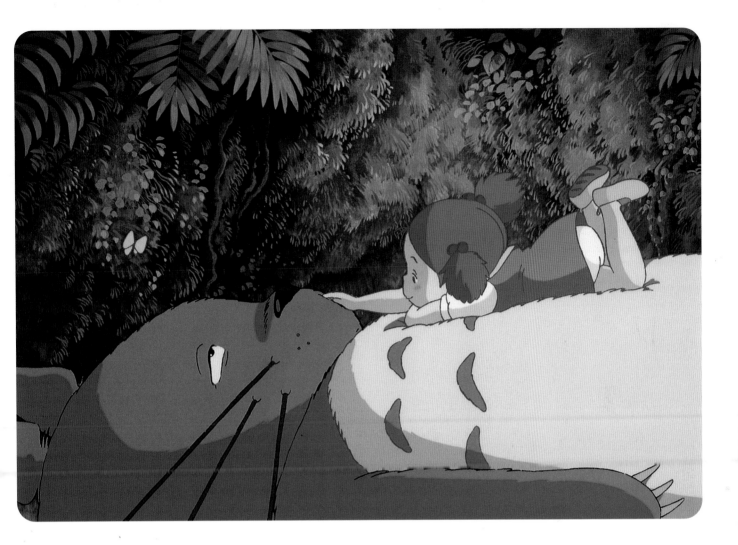

"To-to-ro…? Totoro! So that's your name!"

Mei stretched out comfortably on the fluffy fur. She giggled and repeated the name softly. "Totoro."

Soon Mei's eyes grew heavy too. Before she knew it she had fallen fast asleep on top of Totoro.

When Satsuki came home from school, Mei was nowhere to be found. Satsuki looked for her little sister anxiously. Then she found her hat by the bushes.

"Hey, Dad! Come here, I found Mei's hat!" Satsuki peeked into the bushes and discovered the tunnel. She followed it deeper into the bushes.

The tunnel opened up into a clearing. Satsuki spotted Mei lying on the ground.

"Mei, Mei!" Satsuki called as she shook her sister. Mei woke up and peered about.

"Totoro...Where's Totoro?"

"Totoro?" asked Satsuki.

Dad found his way into the clearing, too.

Mei announced, "I met Totoro. There was a tiny one, and a bigger one, and a HUGE one so big his face was like this!" Mei pulled her cheeks out to show how wide Totoro's mouth was.

"Come on, follow me!" Mei ran farther into the depths of the bushes.

Satsuki and Dad followed, but when they emerged from the tunnel they were back in their own yard.

"That's strange." Mei blinked at the yard as Dad and Satsuki laughed.

"But I really did see Totoro! I'm not lying!" Mei was near tears.

Dad looked gently at Mei and said, "You must have met one of the spirits of the forest. But you can only see them when they want you to. Let's give the forest spirits a proper greeting."

Dad and the girls climbed up a set of stone stairs. Soon they could see the big camphor tree.

"That's the tree!" Mei ran to the tree trunk. She peered down where the hole had been, but, how strange! It was not there.

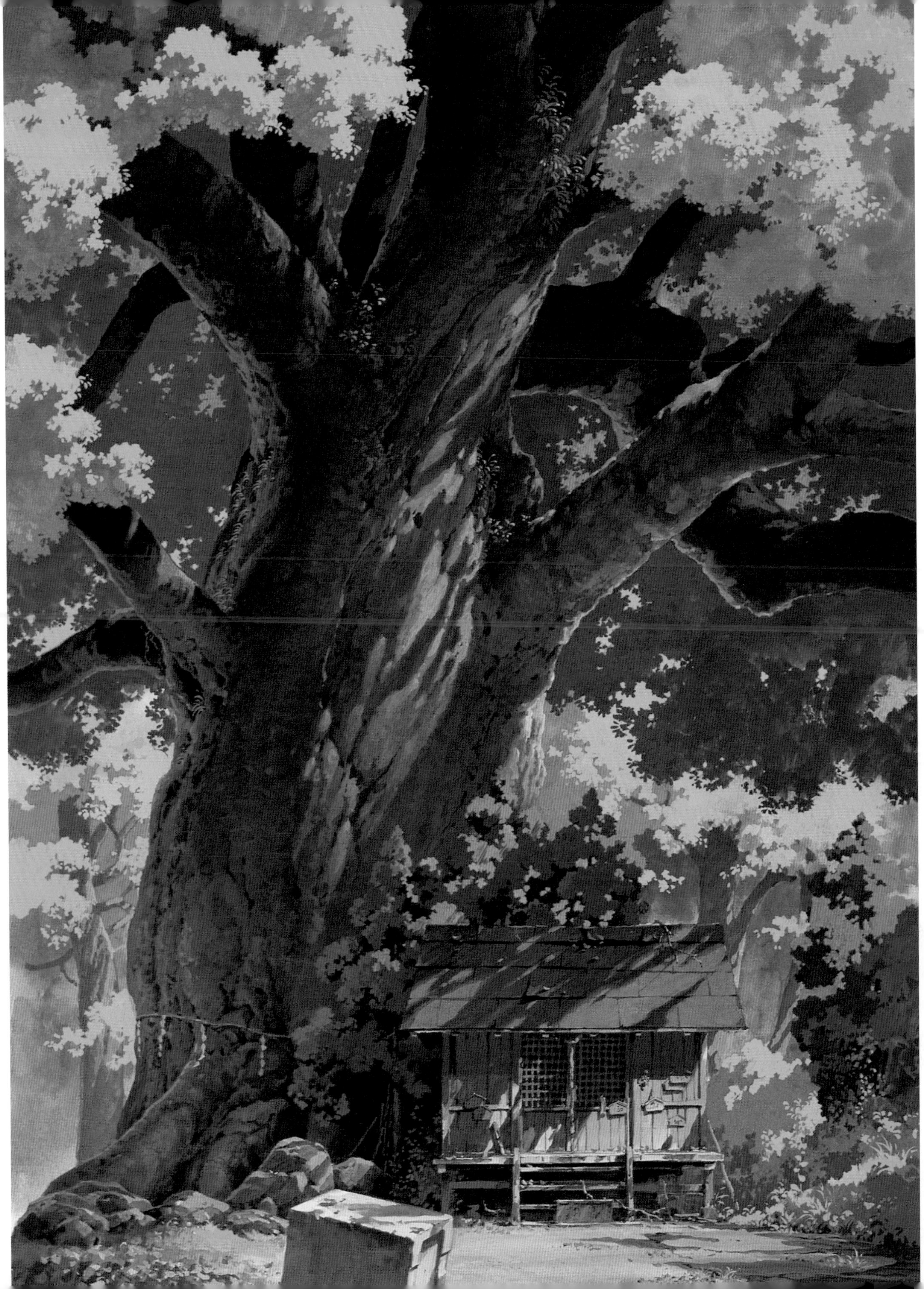

Dad gazed up at the camphor tree. "Hmm. That means the forest spirits don't want to be seen right now."

"What a magnificent tree. It's been around since long ago, back in the time when trees and people used to be friends and protect one another. Let's give this tree a nice greeting."

Satsuki, Mei and Dad bowed in respect to the great camphor tree. "Thank you for watching over Mei. Please continue to look after us," Dad said.

That evening, Satsuki wrote her mother a letter.

"Dear Mom,
We had an exciting day today. Mei met a big forest spirit called Totoro. I
hope I'll be able to see Totoro someday, too…"

Whooo, whooo.

In the distance the night owls hooted.

Totoro's Gift

One rainy evening Mei and Satsuki were waiting at home for Dad.

"Dad left his umbrella here," Satsuki noticed. She glanced at the clock. It was just about time for Dad to come home from his office at the university.

"Let's meet him at the bus stop."

Dad's usual bus arrived at the bus stop, but Dad wasn't on it.

"I wonder what happened. Well, he'll be on the next one for sure," said Satsuki.

It would be a while before the next bus came, but the girls decided to wait.

Mei grew very tired of standing and waiting, and she started to fall asleep.

"I knew this would happen. Here." Satsuki knelt down to let Mei climb on her back. The two kept waiting at the deserted bus stop.

Soon it was dark all around. Satsuki felt very lonely.

Splash, splash, splash…

The sound of footsteps grew nearer.

Someone was standing next to Satsuki.

She glanced out of the corner of her eye, and from below her umbrella she could see a hairy foot with long claws. It was not a human foot!

Satsuki fearfully raised her umbrella and took a look next to her.

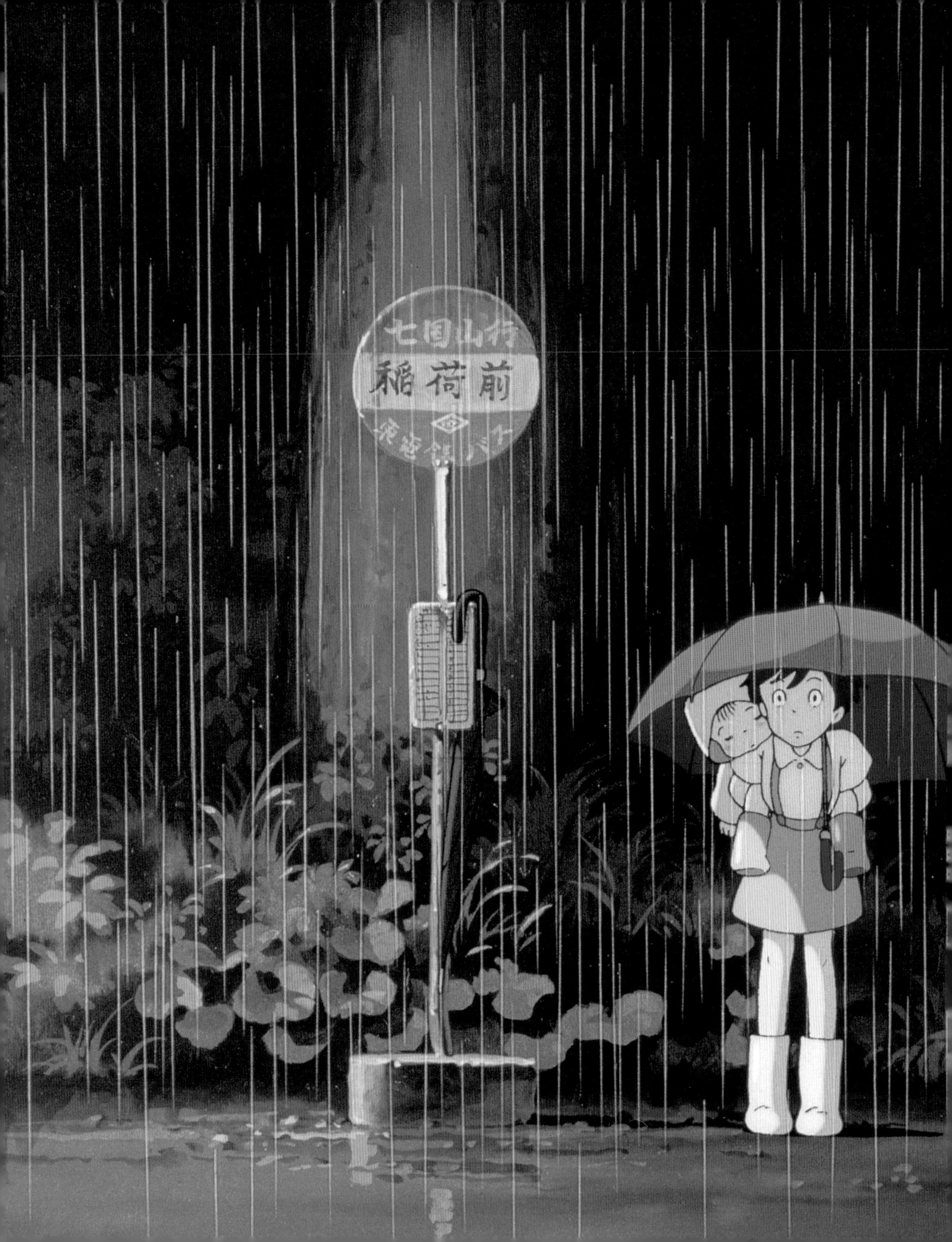
七國山行
稲荷前

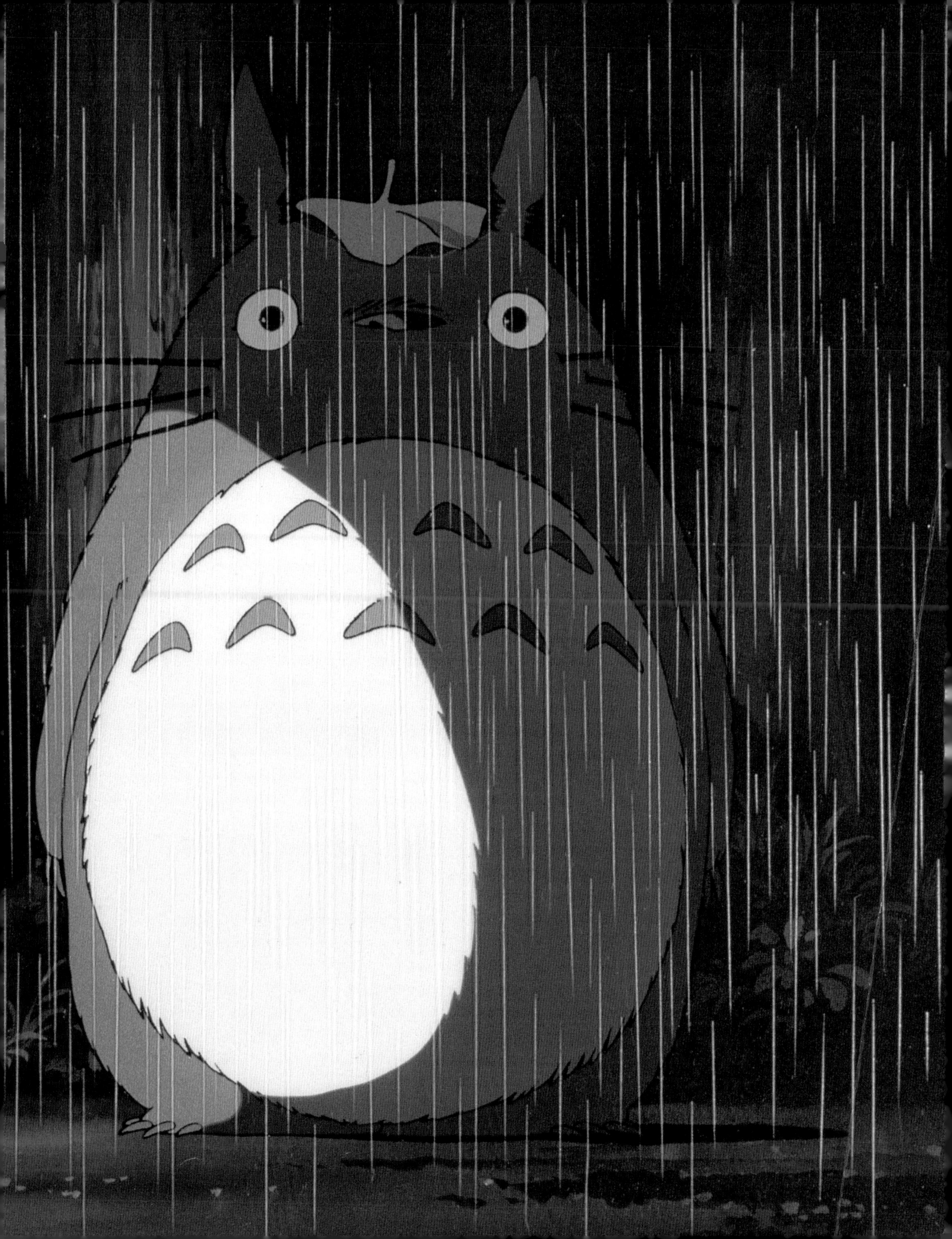

Could it be Totoro? Satsuki's heart was pounding as she took another look.

It must be Totoro! I finally saw Totoro! thought Satsuki. Totoro was wearing a lotus leaf on his head and was soaking wet.

"Here, try this." She handed Totoro her father's umbrella.

Totoro took the umbrella, but didn't seem to know what to do with it. He had never seen an umbrella before.

"Hold it over your head, like this." Satsuki showed Totoro how she was holding hers, and Totoro copied her.

Splat, splat, splat.
Raindrops spilled off the tall tree leaves onto Totoro's umbrella.

Splat, pitterpat.
What splendid sounds! Totoro must have thought the umbrella was a musical instrument.
"Gwahahaha, Gwahahaha," Totoro laughed with delight, jumping up and down.

Thud!
The ground trembled and rainwater poured down from trees all around.

Splat, splat, pitterpat.
Totoro couldn't be happier.

"Gwaaaaaah!" roared Totoro.
Mei woke up.

Just then, a light appeared in the darkness. It looked like the bus was finally coming.

But no, this was no bus. It was a cat.

Wait, it *was* a bus. A gigantic Cat Bus.

The Cat Bus halted at the bus stop. After staring at Satsuki and Mei with its big eyes, it actually grinned.

The two girls couldn't believe it. They were so surprised they couldn't speak.

Totoro held something out. It was a small package wrapped in a bamboo leaf and tied up with a blade of dragon's whisker grass. Mei took it and watched Totoro climb onto the bus.

The twelve legs of the Cat Bus sprang into motion, and the Cat Bus took off at a stunning speed, past the meadows, past the fields....

In no time at all it was out of sight.

"Totoro just took Dad's umbrella," said Satsuki quietly as she stared in shock.

Several days later, Mom got a letter from Satsuki.

"Dear Mom,
We had such a weird, mysterious, spectacular day, my heart is still pounding...."

"As soon as we got home, we opened the present. It was filled with acorns!

We wanted to grow a beautiful forest with the acorns, so we planted them in your garden out back. But they just won't grow."

"Mei watches them all day, every day, waiting for them to sprout. It's starting to make her crabby. Here is a picture of Mei as a crab."

"Summer vacation is almost here. Please get well soon. Love, Satsuki."

Don doko don doko don doko totto…
A mysterious sound woke Satsuki and Mei
up one night.

Don doko don doko don doko totto…
Three Totoros were in their yard.

"Totoro has Dad's umbrella," whispered Mei.

"They're walking right where we planted the acorns," replied Satsuki.
The girls ran outside in their bare feet.

Don doko don doko…

The Totoros were
performing a ritual, bending

and stretching, bending and
stretching in time with the
sound. Satsuki and Mei
joined in.

"Pwaa!" grunted Big Totoro,
stretching up towards the sky
as if to coax something out of
the ground.

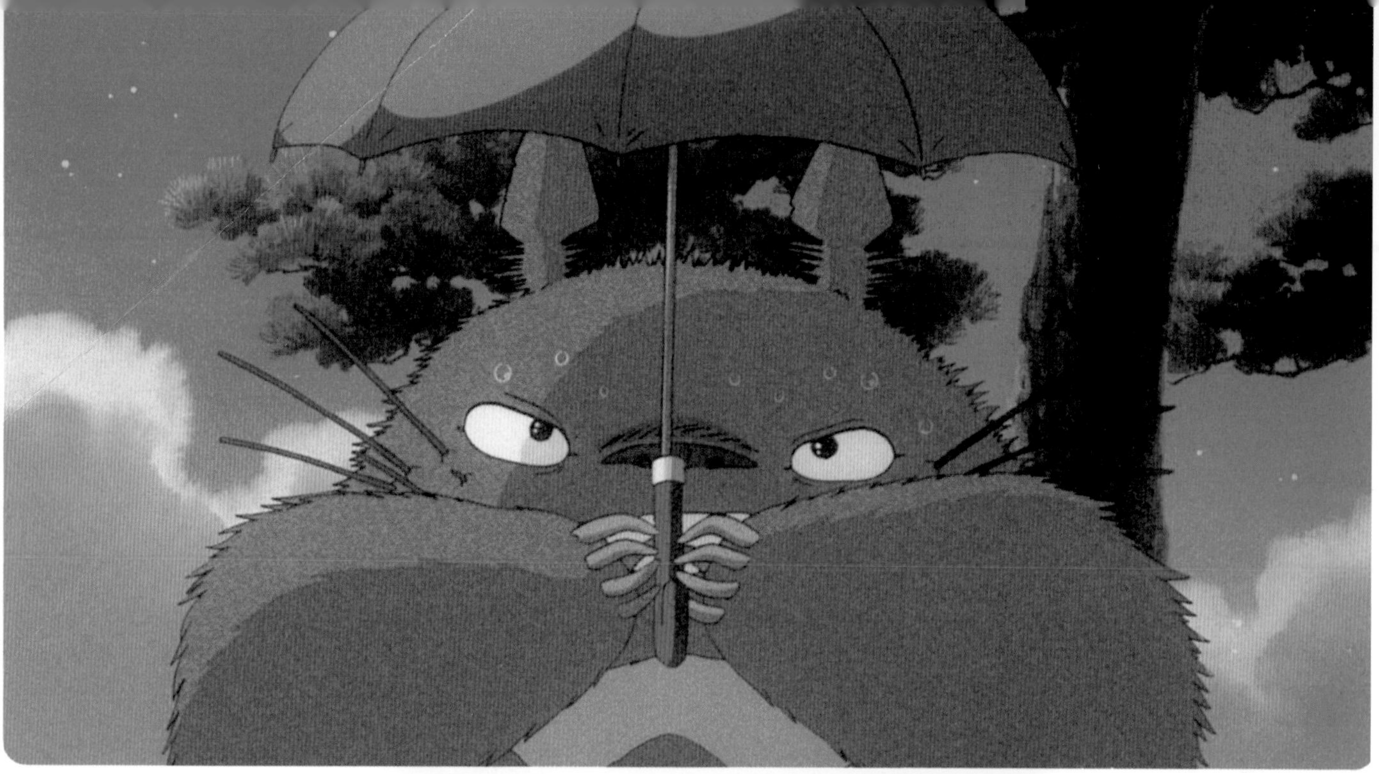
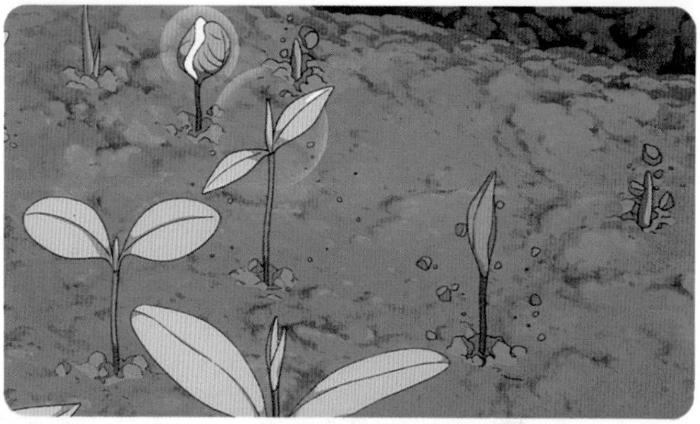
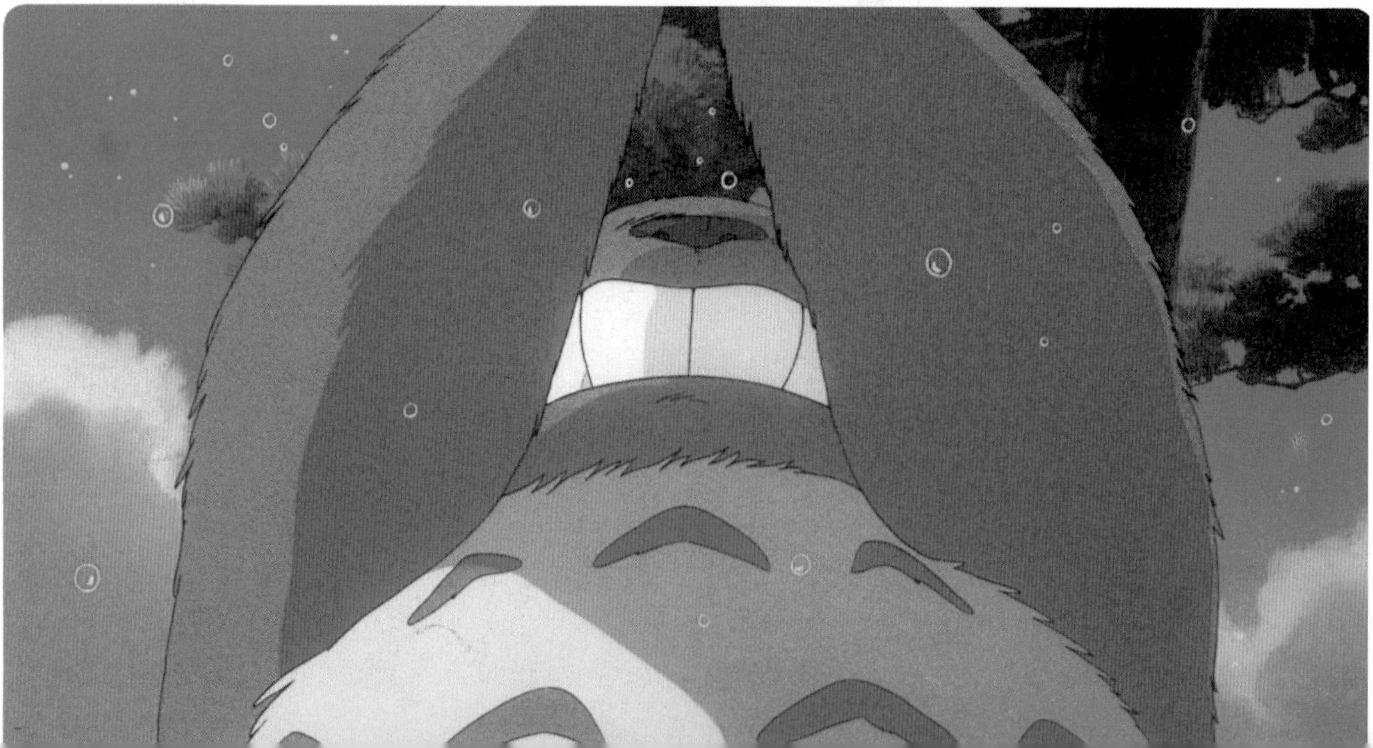

He squatted down deep, then grunted "Pwaah!" again as he stretched up with all his might. And just as he grunted "Pwaah!" a whole bunch of sprouts popped out of the ground.

"Wow!" Satsuki and Mei tried coaxing the plants up, too. Amazingly, each time they stretched up, the plants grew bigger and bigger, becoming trees.

Squat and stretch, squat
and stretch.

*Don doko don doko, grow,
grow, grow!*

The trees shot up towards the
sky, sprouting branches and
leaves until finally all the trees
merged into one enormous tree.

Then Big Totoro pulled out a
top and spun it into the air.

The large top twirled fast. Big
Totoro hopped onto the top
and grinned as if to say,
"Come on!"

One by one, the smaller
Totoros and Satsuki and Mei
jumped onto Big Totoro.

Whirrrrrrr.

The top soared up with the
wind, into the sky.

"Dooooo. Dodorooooooooo. Gwaaaaah," roared Big Totoro. What a splendid night!

Satsuki and Mei roared with glee at the top of their lungs.

"Mei, we're the wind!" laughed Satsuki. And indeed, Big Totoro's roar was just like the roar of the wind.

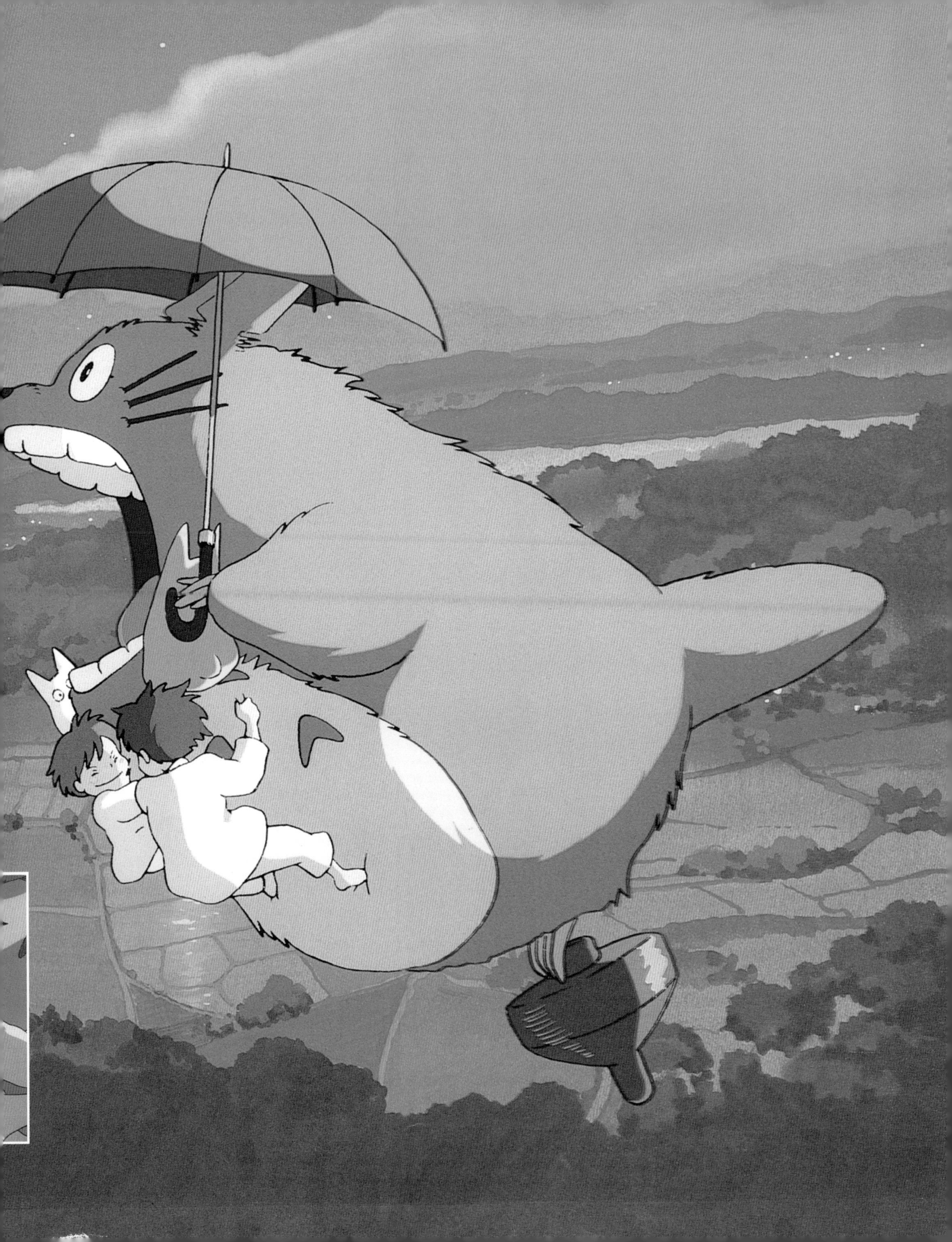

Whoooo, whooo, whooooooo.
At the top of the great
camphor tree, Mei, Satsuki
and the three Totoros

played on ocarina flutes.
The beautiful tones echoed
through the quiet night.

"I hear a lot of owls
tonight," remarked Dad
back at home.
The next morning Satsuki
and Mei leapt out of bed to
see the garden.

"Hmm. Where'd the tree go?"

"Maybe it was all a dream."

But on closer inspection, they noticed rows of small sprouts shining
in the morning sun.

"Hooray! We did it!" cried Satsuki.

"It wasn't a dream!" shouted Mei.

The girls laughed and jumped for joy.

Mei Gets Lost

Summer vacation came. One day the girls went to help Granny pick corn, cucumbers, and tomatoes. It was the day before Mom was to come home, so they were gathering fresh vegetables for her to eat.

"She's getting a lot better, so the doctor said she could come home for two days."

Satsuki and Mei looked so happy they could burst.

Granny nodded and smiled. "We'll feed her lots of my vegetables
while she's here. My vegetables have
soaked up plenty of sunshine, so they're
good for you."

"I'll give her the corn I picked!" declared
Mei.

Just then Kanta came running over holding a telegram.

"It's from Mom's hospital. Something must have happened to her," cried Satsuki worriedly.

"Calm down. First we need to get in touch with your father," replied Granny.

Satsuki and Kanta ran to find a telephone. Mei followed them, still clutching her ear of corn.

Satsuki phoned her father at the university.

"Okay. I'll call the hospital right away," said Dad. "Then I'll call you right back, okay? Just wait by the phone."

Did something happen to Mom? Was she okay? Satsuki's heart was pounding as she waited for her father's call.

When Mei finally caught up, Satsuki had already heard from Dad. She and Kanta were walking sadly back.

"Mom caught a cold, so she doesn't get to come home this weekend."

Mei stopped walking. "No fair!" she shouted.

"It can't be helped, Mei."

"What if she came home early and it made her even worse?"

Mei wouldn't listen. "It's not fair!"

Mei refused to understand. Satsuki's anger and disappointment flared up.

"You want her to die, Mei? Is that what you want?" shouted Satsuki. "You're such a baby! Just grow up!"

"You're so mean!" yelled Mei through her tears.

It was near sunset when Granny came
over to help.

"Don't worry, your father is going to stop
by the hospital. The doctors said your
mom just has a cold. She should be home
next Saturday." Granny did her best to comfort Satsuki.

"This is how it was last time," said Satsuki. "They said Mom just
had a little cold, and she'd be home in a few days. Granny, what will
we do if she dies?"

Satsuki couldn't hold back her tears anymore, and they streamed down her face.

"Sweetheart, don't cry. It's all right."
Granny tried to comfort Satsuki, but the
tears wouldn't stop.

From the house, Mei watched silently.
Then, with a determined look on her face,
she hugged the ear of corn close to her
body and left.

The sun had already begun to set when Satsuki and Granny noticed that Mei was missing.

"I yelled at her this morning. She wanted Mom to come home. I bet she went to see Mom at the hospital. I'll go look!" said Satsuki.

Granny was alarmed. "Kanta! Let everyone know! Mei has disappeared. We need all the help we can get."

Satsuki ran down the road toward the hospital shouting out, "Mei! Mei!"

She asked everyone she met, but nobody remembered seeing her sister. Mei must have gotten lost on her way to the hospital.

Mei, where are you? thought Satsuki. It's my fault. I shouldn't have said such mean things to you…

Satsuki looked at the sun setting over the clouds and fought back tears. She had just started to walk back when Kanta caught up to her.

"Kanta! Find her?"

Kanta shook his head.

"I'll ride my bike to the hospital and look for her. You should go back. They found a sandal in the pond."

"What?!"

"They don't know for sure if it's Mei's..."

Satsuki ran off before he could finish.

"Mei, Mei, don't die!" Satsuki's feet were blistered and bleeding. She took off her sandals and kept running.

She ran and ran until she reached the pond. A crowd of villagers had gathered there.

Granny spotted Satsuki and hurried toward her with a small sandal in her hand.

"Here. Is this Mei's?" Granny's hands trembled.

Satsuki looked carefully at the sandal.

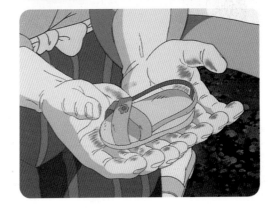

"It's not hers!" said Satsuki. She dropped to her knees in relief. *Thank goodness. But still, where is Mei? What I can do to find her?* A million thoughts crowded Satsuki's mind.

Just then, she glanced up and saw the big camphor tree in the forest.

That's right, she thought. *Totoro.*
Gathering her last bit of strength,
Satsuki started running again, this
time toward the tunnel in the
bushes. It was the tunnel Mei had used when she met Totoro.

Satsuki called out, "Please let me in to see Totoro. Mei's lost." Then
she ran into the tunnel.

Satsuki saw a red light at the end of the
dark tunnel. She ran toward it, but suddenly
her foot got caught on something, and she
tripped.

She tumbled toward the light and landed on
something soft. It was Totoro's big belly.

"Totoro, Mei's lost! Please help me!"

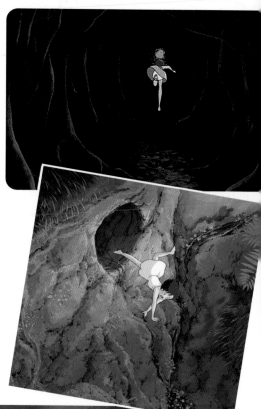

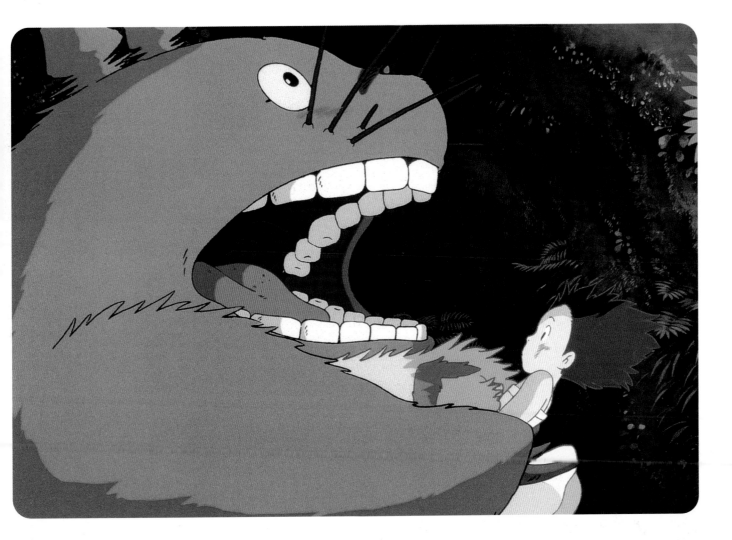

Totoro lifted Satsuki with his big hand.

Gwaaaaah!

With his roar, a strong breeze began to blow, and his body floated up into the air. He carried Satsuki with him, and they floated up to the top of the great tree.

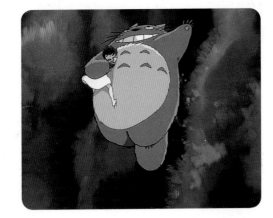

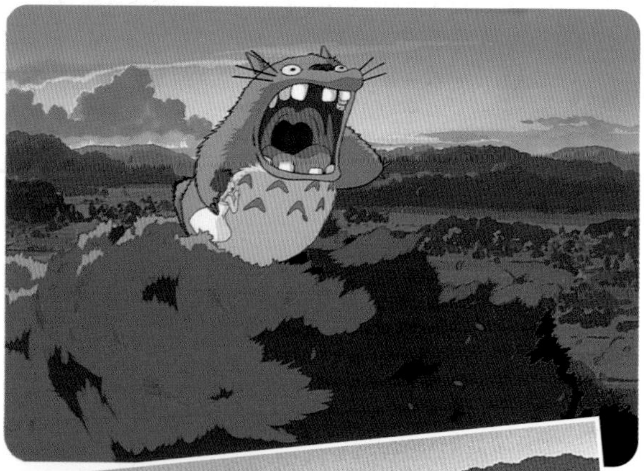

Gwaaaaah!

Totoro let out a huge roar, and from far away something responded.

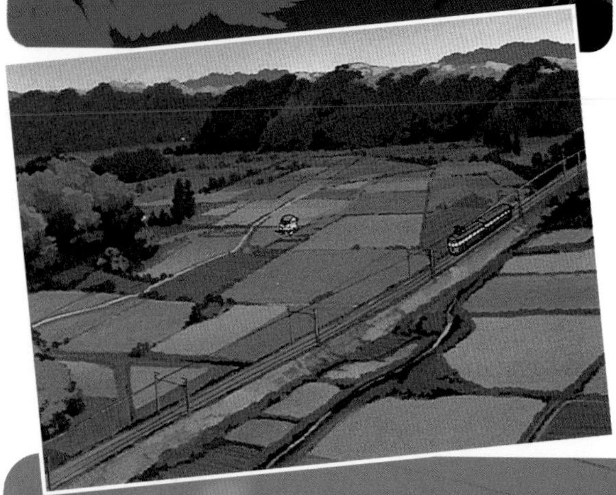

Mrraaaaaaow!

It was the Cat Bus. In the fading light, they could see the Cat Bus racing towards them.

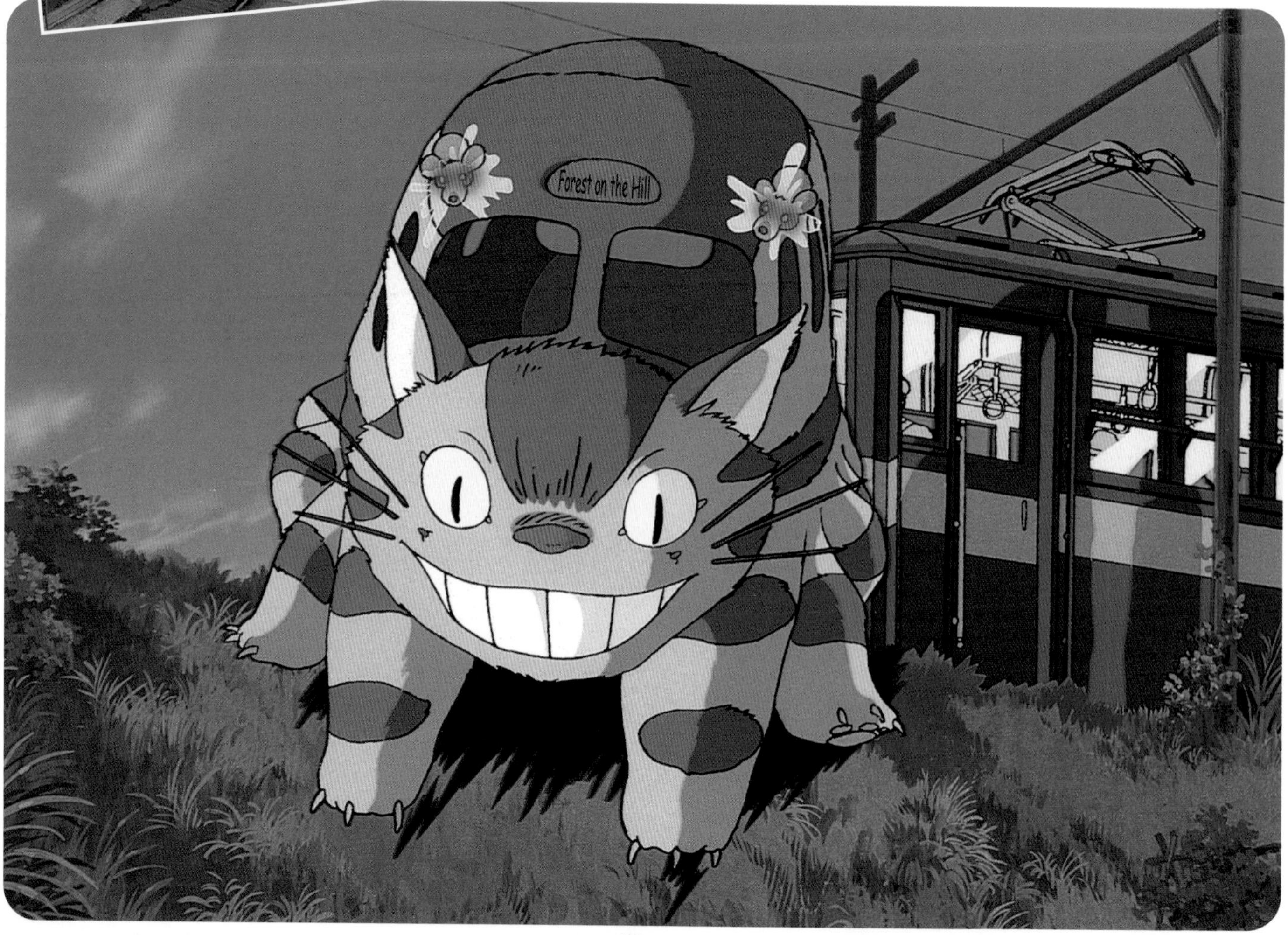
Forest on the Hill

Here and there Satsuki could see the villagers searching for Mei. The Cat Bus sped right by them. Strangely enough, nobody seemed to notice.

"No one else can see it, can they?" Satsuki wondered. She barely had time to be surprised before the Cat Bus clambered up the tree and came to a halt in front of them.

Totoro grunted as if to say, "Get on." Satsuki nervously climbed aboard the Cat Bus. The floor and the chairs felt fluffy and soft like the fur of a cat.

Satsuki read the sign. "Destination…Mei?"

The Cat Bus went racing off.

Through rice fields and meadows, the Cat Bus sped along at an astonishing speed. It even ran on top of power lines.

A long distance away, Mei sat sadly at the feet of some stone Ojizosama, Japanese spirits that protect children. She was completely exhausted.

From somewhere came her sister's voice, calling, "Mei!"

Mei stood up. "Satsuki! Where are you?" The tears she had been holding back now streamed down her face.

"Mei, over here!"

Mei looked up in the direction of
Satsuki's voice and was amazed. She was
so surprised she even stopped crying.

Mei stared as the
Cat Bus took a
flying leap off
the power lines
and landed right in
front of her.

"Mei!"

"Satsuki!"

The sisters hugged each other tightly. "Were you trying to take your corn to Mom at the hospital?" Satsuki asked.

Mei nodded.

The sign on the Cat Bus had changed. It now read,
"Shichikokuyama Hospital."

"You're going to take us to the hospital?" gasped Satsuki. "Thank
you!" She gave the Cat Bus a big hug, and the Cat Bus purred.

All aboard for the hospital!
The Cat Bus took off,
leaping over fields and
mountains.

In a moment they had arrived. The Cat Bus landed in a tree right by the hospital. The girls could see their mother and father through the window.

"Mom looks okay," said Satsuki with relief.

"Yeah, Mommy and Daddy are laughing," said Mei.

"We'd better head back. Everyone's worried about you."

A gentle breeze wafted into the hospital room.

"Hmm?" Mom looked around. "I thought I just heard Satsuki and Mei's voices." Her eyes fell on an ear of corn resting on the windowsill.

Dad picked it up, saying, "Maybe you did. Look at this."

"For Mommy"

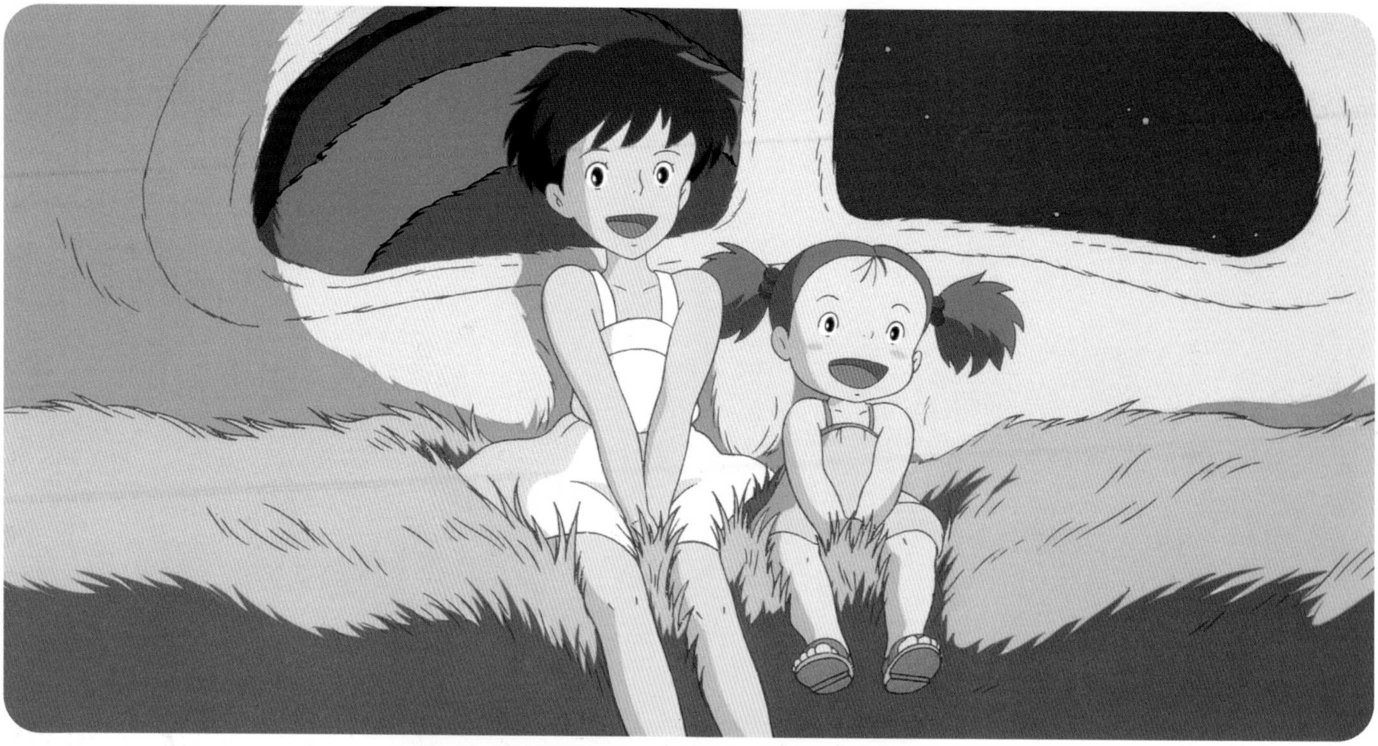

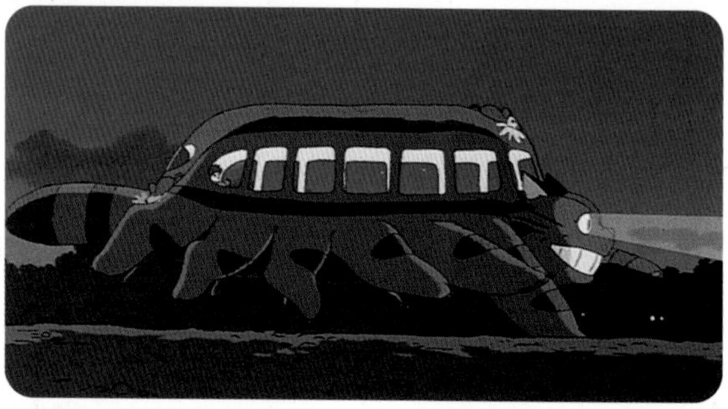

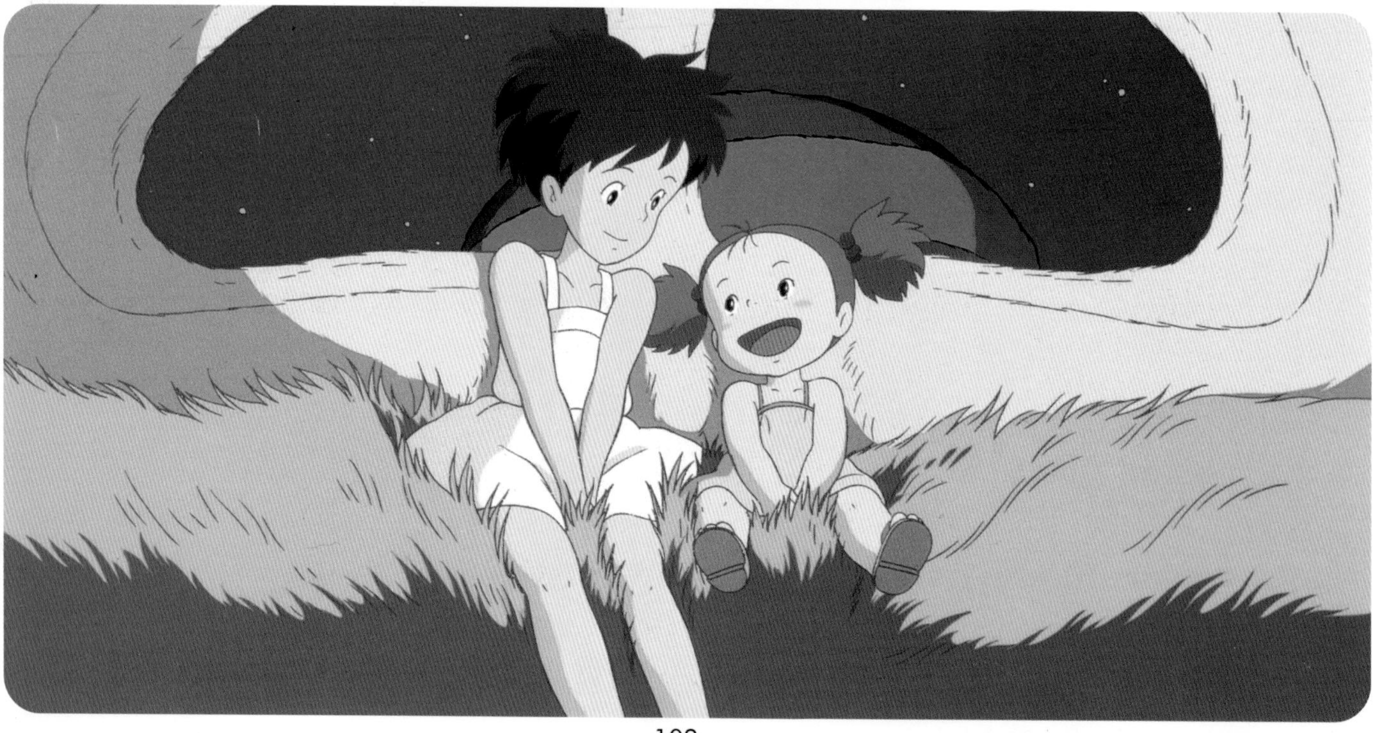

The Cat Bus swayed gently as it carried Satsuki and Mei home.

"Thank you very much," said Satsuki.

"Bye-bye! See you again!" called out Mei.

The Cat Bus grinned and disappeared into the night sky.

Down the road, Granny and Kanta were walking home. Mei ran towards them. "Granny!"

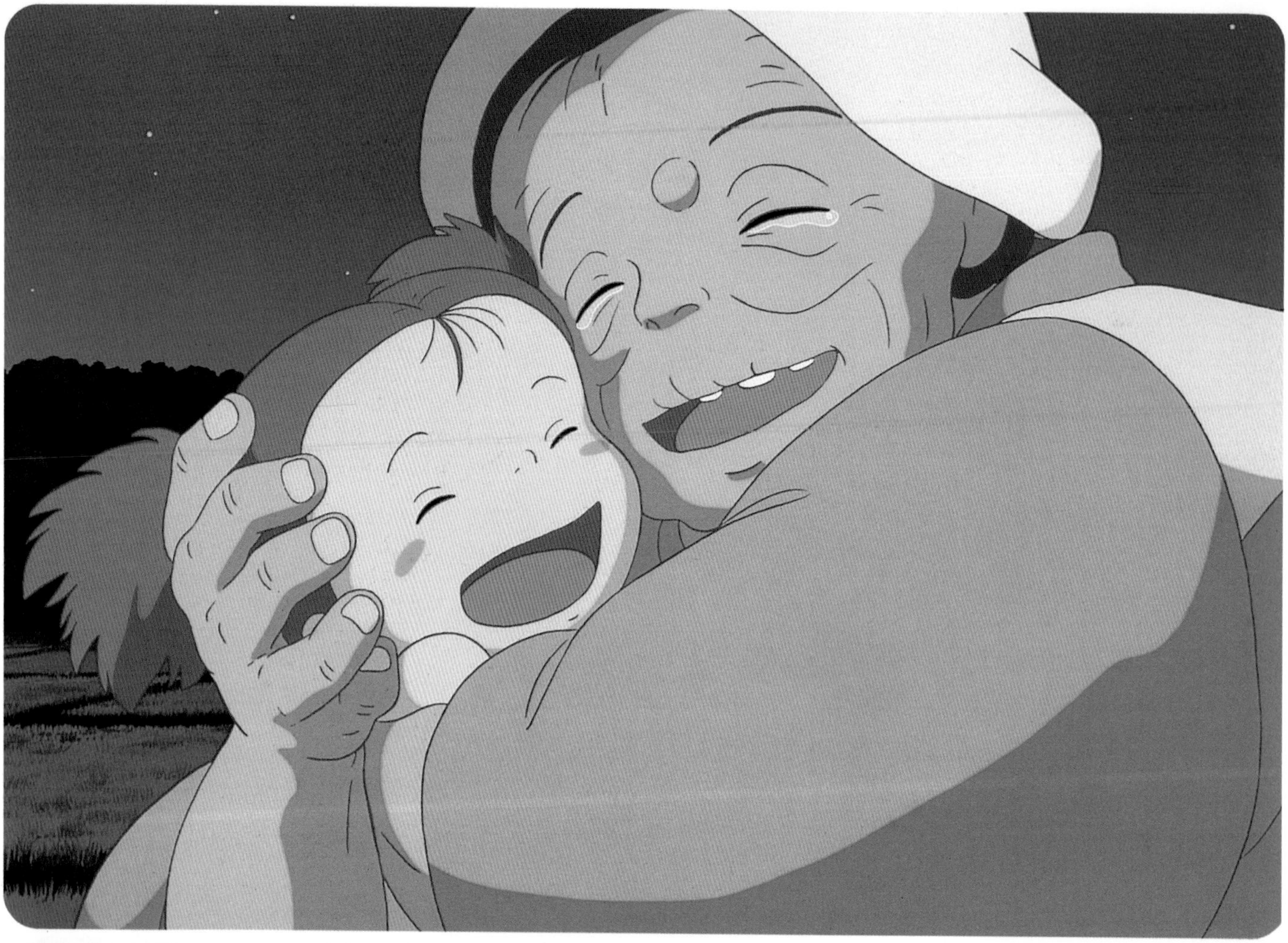

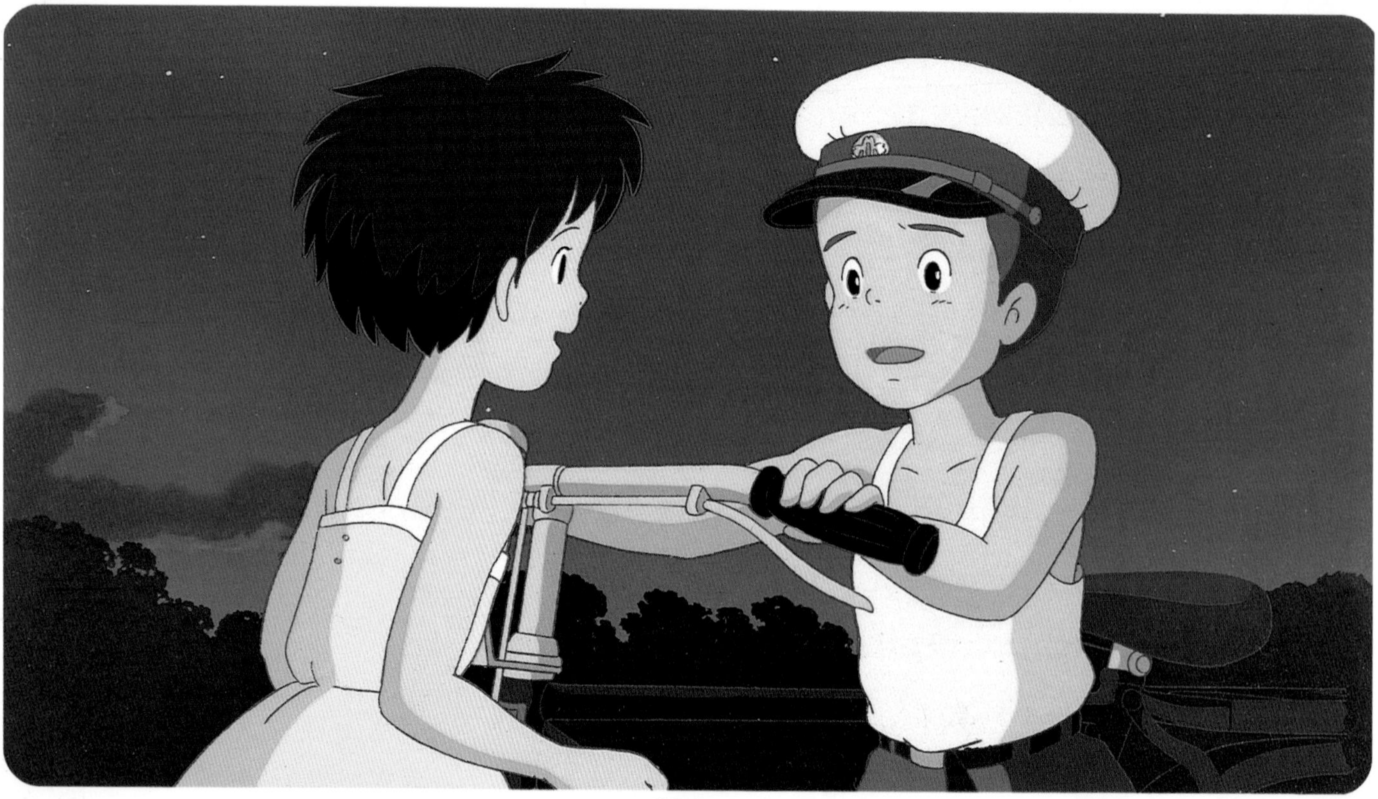

"Thank goodness. Thank goodness. We were so worried." Granny's eyes filled with tears as she hugged Mei.

"Thank you, Kanta," said Satsuki. Kanta laughed, looking embarrassed.

Whoooo, whoooo, whoooo.
Up above, the Totoros blew their ocarinas.
The soft tones echoed through the
beautiful starlit sky.

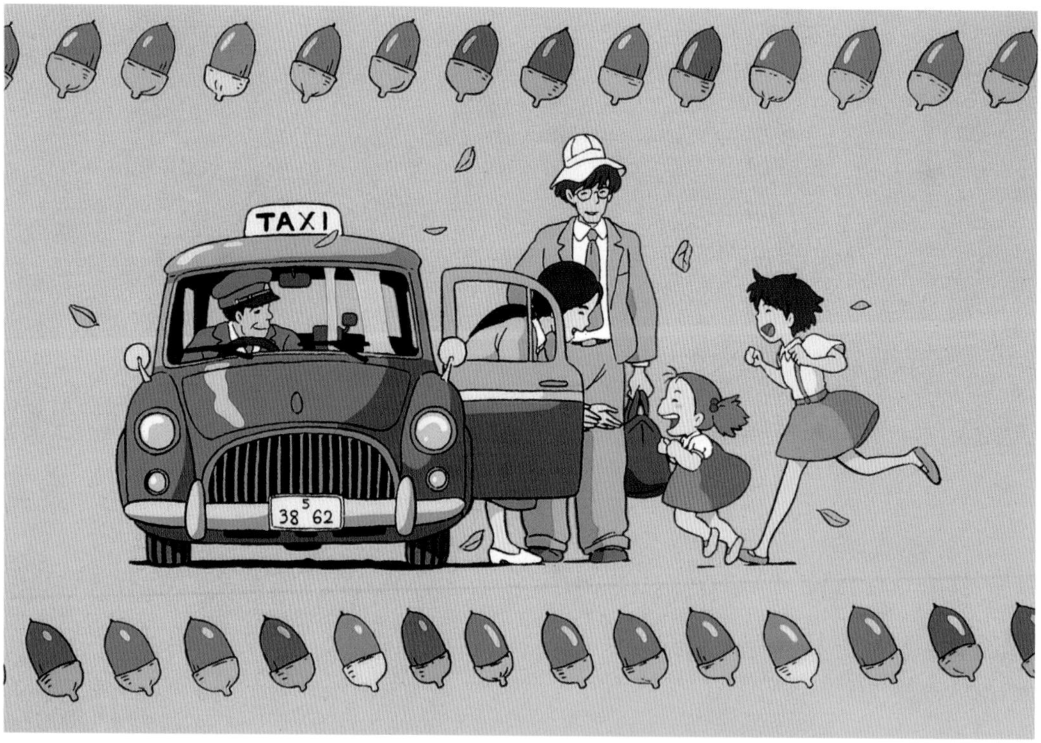
TAXI
5
38 62

THE END

Satsuki and Mei met Totoro and the Cat Bus here while waiting for their father.

The neighborhood where Satsuki went to find a telephone to tell her father about the hospital telegram.

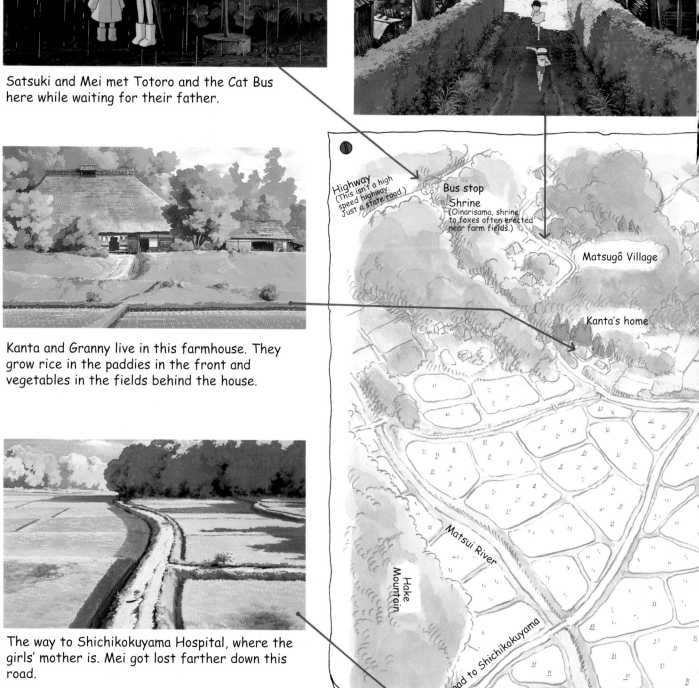

Kanta and Granny live in this farmhouse. They grow rice in the paddies in the front and vegetables in the fields behind the house.

The way to Shichikokuyama Hospital, where the girls' mother is. Mei got lost farther down this road.

Highway
(This isn't a high speed highway. Just a state road.)

Bus stop

Shrine
(Oinarisama, shrine to foxes often erected near farm fields.)

Matsugô Village

Kanta's home

Matsui River

Hake Mountain

Road to Shichikokuyama

Satsuki and Mei's new home. The villagers used to call it "the haunted house," because nobody had lived there for a long time.

Totoro Map

Totoro lives in the big camphor tree at the top of this forest.

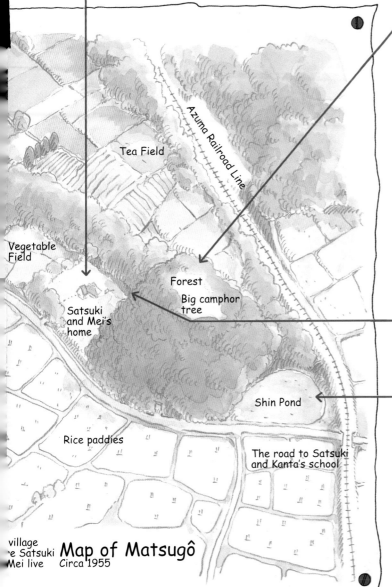

Azuma Railroad Line

Tea Field

Vegetable Field

Forest

Big camphor tree

Satsuki and Mei's home

Shin Pond

Rice paddies

The road to Satsuki and Kanta's school

village e Satsuki Mei live

Map of Matsugô

Circa 1955

The tunnel in the bushes is around here.

The pond where a sandal was found, the day Mei got lost.

Afterword
By Rieko Nakagawa
Children's Author

Perhaps someday, somewhere, you too will be able to see a Totoro.

I saw *My Neighbor Totoro* on the big screen in a movie theater. In the dark I couldn't make out who was sitting in the packed room, but it was clear that everyone was watching intently, enraptured by what they saw. From here and there I heard the innocent laughter of children and their cute "oohs" of surprise. Those sounds drew me in, and I enjoyed myself even more. Stirred by both the screen and the audience, I felt my sputtering senses awaken. It had been quite a while since I'd so enjoyed the atmosphere only movie theaters can provide.

This feeling of happiness and satisfaction stayed in my heart long after seeing the film. In fact, just a few minutes ago as I was cooking in the kitchen I found myself singing, "Arukoo, arukoo, watashi wa genki." ["Let's go, let's go. Let's go walking you and me."] It was Mei's song.

When I chop vegetables or stir pots, my mind is usually free to contemplate enjoyable things. These days, it's always *My Neighbor Totoro*.

As I boil spinach I think, "Totoro is so fun, so amusing, so impressive!" "Big Totoro is around seven feet tall, they say. What on earth is a Totoro?" I muse to myself. As I grind sesame in the mortar, I reflect that Totoro is said to have lived in the forests of Japan for thousands of years. My imagination is invigorated as I think about how they are not so much ghostly spirits as they are messengers of the gods.

As I imagine this and that, I come to realize that although that particular camphor tree was enormous indeed, I too have my own memories of that country scenery. I begin to feel nostalgic, as if I were Satsuki. And I have distinct memories of moving day and that mountain of luggage piled high on a truck traveling a bumpy country road, the haunted house in Matsugo Village, surrounded by green forests, the awkward yet kind Kanta, the resilient Granny, the path to school, the road to Shichikokuyama, the pond, the views by the Matsui River, that rainy day, the meeting with Totoro at the bus stop with a stone-heavy Mei on my back, the commotion when Mei was lost, and the ride on the Cat Bus. How wonderful when things I see in a movie begin to feel like my own memories.

I'm sure it wasn't just me. I bet everyone who saw the film thought of the places dear to them and recalled many memories.

— Children will probably climb trees and explore the backs of shrines, all in the hopes of meeting Totoro. And when they see thick forests and distant mountaintops, they will wonder if Totoro is doing well and feel a longing to send their greetings.

Totoro creator Hayao Miyazaki said, "I wanted to make *My Neighbor Totoro* in the heartfelt belief that the things we've forgotten, the things we haven't noticed, and the things we've given up as lost all still do exist." I am sure that young people keenly sense this.

Now if I may be allowed to comment on the film in my own fashion, I would say that *My Neighbor Totoro* is a true story that actually took place on the outskirts of Tokyo around 1955. From start to finish, I just do not think this is a made-up story.

The old house where the Kusakabe family

lived really existed. The entryway, the hallways, the stairs, kitchen, and bath…they were all just so. Those mysterious *susuwatari* that Satsuki and Mei found…they did exist. You see, my house had them too. They dwelled in the dark corners of the kitchen and the dirt-floored rooms and disappeared when we had big cleanings.

Totoro really existed, too. Or rather, it was simply a matter of fact that there were Totoros in the forest. They lived peaceful, carefree lives in the hollows of ancient trees and caves, but they usually could not be seen by humans. The fact that Satsuki and Mei saw them indicates there was some kind of understanding between them. Perhaps someday, somewhere, you too will be able to see a Totoro.

It is also true that there was a Cat Bus. It ran wildly and recklessly, providing delightful thrills. I believe it still races about between skyscrapers, but with all those neon signs around it is hard to make out.

How hard it must have been in those days for Tatsuo Kusakabe to care for fourth grader Satsuki and four-year-old Mei while his wife Yasuko was hospitalized. But he never grumbled or fussed. It is true. And the girls stayed strong and were a great help to him. It must have been hardest on Yasuko, but she always had a warm smile on her face, a smile that sustained the hopes of Satsuki and Mei. Thus, the family prevailed splendidly through difficult circumstances. They were a warm and kind family. Ideal neighbors. Nineteen fifty-five seems like just a short while ago to me, yet at the same time it feels like ancient history. In any case, we have experienced rapid change all around us since then. Even now, as modernization and industrialization continues to progress, daily life becomes ever more convenient and luxurious. So are we happier now than thirty years ago? I can't say we are. What do we truly love? What do we truly cherish?

My Neighbor Totoro has an answer: the beauty of nature and its changing seasons.

Rieko Nakagawa graduated from the Tokyo Metropolitan Advanced Institute for Preschool Teaching and wrote stories for a children's literature group "Itadori" while working as a nursery school teacher. In 1962, she published The No-No Nursery School *(Fukuinkan Shoten) and was awarded the Ministry of Health and Welfare Award, the Sankei Children's Book Award, and many others. In 1980,* Koinu no Roku ga Yattekita *[Here Comes Roku, the Puppy] (Iwanami Shoten) was awarded the Mainichi Publishing Culture Award. Major works include* Kaeru no Eruta *[Eruta the Frog](1964),* Momoiro no Kirin *[The Pink Giraffe](1965),* The Blue Seed*(1967), and the well-loved* Guri to Gura *series.*

BASED ON THE STUDIO GHIBLI FILM

ORIGINAL STORY AND SCREENPLAY WRITTEN AND DIRECTED BY
HAYAO MIYAZAKI

English Adaptation/Naoko Amemiya
Design & Layout/Izumi Evers
Editor/Megan Bates

VP, Publishing/Alvin Lu
VP, Sales & Product Marketing/Gonzalo Ferreyra
VP, Creative/Linda Espinosa
Publisher/Hyoe Narita

My Neighbor Totoro (Tonari no Totoro) © 1988 Nibariki – G
All rights reserved.
First published by Tokuma Shoten Co., Ltd. in Japan.
My Neighbor Totoro logo © 2004 Buena Vista Home Entertainment, Inc.

Printed in China

Published by VIZ Media, LLC
295 Bay St.
San Francisco, CA 94133

First printing, October 2005
Third printing, December 2009

Visit www.viz.com